After
Texas
Sank

A Novel

by
Larry Murley

Illustrated by
Kerry Kelly

www.larrymurley.com

www.facebook.com/AfterTexasSank

After Texas sank, I started remembering more of the things that the Old Man talked about. No one actually believed that half the United States would just up and disappear, but the Old Man had mentioned that it was a possibility. Yeah, but he was just an old man. I thought he was pretty cool though. He would stand up to anyone. He hated to see people waste their lives following false ideals.

But when Texas started mimicking the Titanic, I realized just maybe he might be right about some other things that he expounded. I was about 22 when I met him. Funny, I don't remember exactly the first time I saw him, but I sure remember the first time I became aware of him. It was 1990. Remember, I was 22. I was pretty sure that I had accumulated all the knowledge that a young male human would ever need, and I was probably invulnerable. Yeah, right.

Anyway, I proceeded to ride my motorcycle through this crowd of people. It was fun to watch them give me space. I had just made my second pass and was about to turn around to do it again when this hand reached out and literally plucked me right off the seat. I hit the ground like a rock, and jarred every bone in

my body. I tasted blood from biting my tongue. Then man, I saw red! I came up ready for war.

Standing in front of me was this old guy. Kinda balding, but a pretty big dude. He reached out and openhanded just set me back on my butt.

"Young Man," he said, "Why don't you just sit there and remember your manners?"

It wasn't really a question I realized, but more of an order, something I didn't believe in taking.

He squatted in front of me and looking directly in to my eyes. "I live just over there in that trailer. When you get yourself together, come see me and pick up your scooter."

I watched him as he walked over and picked up my bike and walked it toward the the vacant lot where a large trailer was parked.

"I'm going to get him," I muttered through aching teeth.

"Better forget it," said a ragged guy in a cammy jacket, "he will have you for lunch. Go talk to him. Might be hell of a time to learn something!"

The rest is history. I went and reclaimed my motorcycle and wound up spending a couple of hours just talking. I found out there was no animosity in the old man. He just felt like when something was wrong it was his job to straighten it out. Funny though, life seemed to get serious for me after that. Maybe it was just coincidence, but I don't think so. I think I was ready and my teacher had appeared.

It was just two or three days after the millennium. I was in Austin, standing on a street corner listening to a Jesus Preacher ranting about the state of our existence. A large hand appeared on my shoulder.

"See, I told you the Y2K bug wouldn't really bite. But don't let down you guard. Right there lies one of our real dangers." Pointing at the preacher, the old man sighed. "They will destroy us yet."

I had heard him speak of the moral majority as being a College of Knowledge based on eternal misdirection. I wasn't sure where he came from on this for many years. I don't think the old man was anti-religion or anti-God, I think he just saw the dangers in fundamentalism regardless of the source.

Somehow, when you know something down deep inside you, you just have to justify it with words or facts. I experienced this a couple of times in my life before it ever became a realization.

The old man often said that life was like one of those huge jigsaw puzzles that was real popular in the last millennium. The way he put it went something like this. If you remain aware of the things around you, the Secrets of the Universe will just fall like snowflakes in the fall. And if you will watch closely, they will fall in their proper place and the more of these that you see, the more clearer the picture will become. Pretty soon you will catch your self thinking, after observing one of these snowflakes, *Wow!! Now that makes sense. Why didn't I think of that before?*

I learned to appreciate history. No, not the kind you learned in school - dry dates and boring facts that seemed that only a lawyer could have quoted, and usually tainted by what ever color the reigning power wished to color it. His history was the journals and diaries and stories of his personal predecessors and their neighbors and acquaintances. Somehow, these seemed to give a clearer picture of the past.

He said, "Son, (it made no difference that our blood was not linked, almost any man of any age difference was 'son'), a seer without a knowledge of the past would have no idea what his vision contained."

In 2001 I hung mostly in Texas, doing odd jobs, small construction jobs, etc. I used to go to Austin about every other weekend to party, and mostly to listen to music. Austin was a very exciting place to me. Music, nite life, liberal attitudes, and some of the prettiest girls in the whole world. There is something different about Texas women. Or there was. Well, at least some survived.

That seems so long ago somehow. It seems only in our era that a specific place in the world can exist only in your memory. I listen now for people telling stories around the campfires when communities meet to trade or to be social, pictures painted of a starry night of a weekend at Padre Island, or of the freeways in California. The young listen in wonder, and wish for the good old days. Still, the world seems larger now than it did then.

There must have been many that could see

things were going to change, but I think it was only a few that realized it was going to be so drastic.

The New Year had passed without any real changes in my world and life went on more or less as usual. It didn't get any better. Fuel was up. The tech world was probably the thing that expanded more than any other. But even the old people recognized the drastic difference in the attitudes of the masses and the speed at which we rode the daily roller coaster.

Since I had not seen the old man in a year or so, I decided to take a little trip to Colorado. It was early spring and the blue bonnets were in full bloom. Looking across the prairie west of Brenham, Texas it was a sea of blue with occasional brush stokes of rust, making one think that the red clay had splashed itself into natures picture. A pretty picture, one that would be hard to recall in later weeks when the hot sun would turn all but the pine trees to brown.

Up ahead on the edge of Giddings a young man in leather jacket and moccasins and blue hair stood trying to look his most respectable self, hoping someone would stop for him. Oh Hell, why not?

"Hi. Where you headed?"

"West."

"No Shit."

"Actually, Abilene."

"Get in."

"Kewl."

"I'm Jeff Bartlett."

"I'm David Suttle."

We rode for several miles with out talking.

Finally I asked, "What's in Abilene?"

"My Father. He had a stroke."

"Too bad. Is he going to be ok?"

"I don't know. They don't have a phone. I just gotta get there."

"I understand."

Later that afternoon we turned off on the narrow dirt road into an equally narrow driveway toward an aging mobile home more or less surrounded by junk cars and other collectables. As we approached, a graying woman some where in her forties to sixties stepped through the torn screen door into the fading light. Her face went from a worried mask of confrontation to joy as she recognized the young man with me. She sighed, "Thank God!"

I had walked out to the corner of the yard to stretch my legs and to enjoy the setting of the sun over the brushy hills to the west. I stood for sometime catching the last rays of sunshine. Sensing someone near I turned. It was my young passenger.

"How is he?"

He looked down. "He is dying."

I felt a pang of sadness. I had lost my parents when i was about twelve, and I knew what he must be feeling.

He looked up. "So, thanks a lot for bring me here. I wish I could pay you, but....... I'm afraid I don't have much to offer."

"Do something good for someone sometime soon," I said, "that will be pay enough. Oh, by the way, I am on my way to Colorado to meet a mentor of mine. If you are ever up around Fort Collins come look me up. Now I must be off. Good luck."

I gave him my name and the old man's address.

The next day I drove up a rocky drive above Horseshoe Lake. Parking my car, I walked the next 50 yards down to the weathered old trailer. As I rounded the corner I heard "I was expecting you yesterday."

I replied, "I had to do a good deed."

"That's good. You can't hardly ever stack up enough of them. Come give me a hug."

I never could explain, even to myself, what effect he had on me. He was cranky, but gentle. He always seemed without saying anything to make me want to achieve more than I was capable of, and indeed, I would find myself doing that, seemingly without effort.

One time I questioned him about that. He answered, "Maybe sometimes it is enough for at least one of us to know that you can, reckon?"

It was true though. Good deeds need to be stacked up, 'cause you are probably gonna always need more than you seem to give.

I remember once, back in the late 80's, I met this Vietnamese guy in Houston. We were both studying for our GED. He because he needed to finish his education, me because I had neglected to finish school. I found out he was walking incredible distances to get his certificate, so I would pick him up when I could and let him ride with me.

One day he told me his story about how he escaped from Vietnam, and about his journey to America. I was flabbergasted. I had never heard of that kind of hardship. I felt pretty lame for all the excuses and complaints I had piled up over the years.

I guess that is what always drew me back. That and the fact I was more able to see the important things more clearly. Like living simply and close to the earth. The old man didn't like cities. He said that cities were the scourge of our planet. Indeed, of our civilization he talked about the effect of the heat they created with their miles of concrete and metal and asphalt and the reflective effect on the eco-system around them, the pollution of their waste. He said that if society had any chance at all, it would be when the cities were abandoned and people live in small tribal societies again. I have always wondered if he had any vision of what was to happen in the next 20 or so years.

After we had visited for a while he got up and beckoned. "Son, I have got something to show you. Let's take a ride."

We got into his old 4x4 and drove to an area about 25 mile from Fort Collins. Up graded county roads, picturesque in their grassy meadows with their pile of stacked rocks, left as if some giant child had been arranging the countryside. Up above us to the west ribbons of snow laced the high peaks of the northern most Colorado Rockies. We passed through a couple of ranches and a couple of gates and time slowed as it always did as we left civilization behind us.

We stopped at the bottom of a steep hill. He put the old truck into four-wheel drive, then we ground our way up the mountainside. About a quarter of a mile later and 600 ft higher in elevation we topped the hill and a beautiful vista lay before us. Acres of meadows dotted with pines and a few aspens sprawled down and out beyond lay the great plains. He pulled the truck out of four-wheel and we turned to the right up a narrow dirt road into the forest. About a quarter mile later he pulled off to the right, killed the engine, and said, "Come here." We walked about a hundred feet to the edge of a very steep canyon.

The view was fabulous. I could see for miles all around.

"Son, I want you to buy this property. It is probably the most important thing you could ever do for yourself."

The rest is history. We arranged the purchase and about a month later the place was mine.

The next 5 years were a whirlwind of moving, building, creating. The old mans energy never seemed to wain. He was full of ideas and suggestions, and he worked like it was his own.

April 30th, 2006

It was spring. I woke up one morning listening to the local college radio station. The news person seemed agitated, and upset. As I listened, a story unfolded. The President of the United States, a prominent member of the "moral majority" had just signed into law a bill forcing all children in public schools, both here and in foreign countries to start their school days with prayers. And the prayers were to be to the Christian deities. No other religion was to be recognized.

The Islamic world and the Government of China had reacted with a violent protest burning churches and synagogues the world over. The

Congress and the President countered by putting the U.S. Military on active alert. The broadcast cut to a government official who was bemoaning that the Christian religion had been proven to be the only religion with a live God and the rest of the world would have to just get used to it. The other religions founders like Buddha and Mohammed were only teachers. In the background, you could hear a strain of *Onward Christian Soldiers*.

I felt a queasy feeling in my stomach and one of those snowflakes fell into place. The old man may be right. He said it would be dangerous if they got into power around the millennium.

The next few days rumors and threats and discontent ranged at large. Threats were made by both sides. We all knew we were going to war, we just didn't know what direction. I hoped it wouldn't be China.

Reports came from L.A. and San Francisco and Atlanta of riots and clashes between Christian fundamentalists and other factions, some of them weren't even particularly religious.

Years went by. One day in early 2015 I decided to go to town for supplies. As I drove the 25 miles to Fort Collins I marveled, for the hundredth time at least, how much my world changed in those 25 or so miles. Up there at my place on the edge of the National Forest life was real and, in spite of the technology that I enjoyed, still simple. Down in town people were in a hurry to be nowhere, and for the most part damn rude about it. If they could have only known what the next few years would bring.

Parking my truck on College Avenue in front of the Ace Hardware, I proceeded to wander toward Old Town Square. It was always enjoyable to wander through the shops and hangout in the pubs and restaurants and listen to people talk. I missed that a lot up in the hills.

I spent the better part of an hour feeding my social side and enjoying food not prepared for oneself, and decided to get back to the hardware store and the reason for making the trip to town.

As I passed the local Radio Shack a reporter was excitedly reporting a military coup in Russia protesting the new Prime Minister that had just gained power. She went on to say that in the excitement of the attempted takeover, several nuclear missiles were reported missing.

Driving back that evening, that news disturbed me. I wondered where the weapons would show up.

Next morning, as I pumped my water tank up for the day and watched a 'goldie' glide on the wind over the canyon below my camp, my phone buzzed in my ear.

I answered, "Hello?"

The soft voice answered, "You miss me?"

My whole being turned on.

"I hope you are telling me that you are only 15 minutes away. I don't think I could last much longer."

"Well.....I will be home tonight. But my connection in Dallas didn't connect. By the way, have you caught the news this morning?"

The sudden hiss of water coming through the vent cap of the water tank suddenly brought me back to reality. I reached quickly and shut off the switch to the pump and closed the valve.

Answering, "No, what's up?"

I was really more interested on getting her warm body back up the mountain than in studying current events. But it was good just to hear her voice, regardless what she was saying.

As she proceed to tell me the delay in her flight was mostly a direct result of the riots, and lastly the stolen missiles were reported to be out of Russia and missing. A huge search was being carried out by all governments everywhere. Scary.

My mate, Nell, had flown to Austin a week ago to attend a sick relative and by now was sorely missed. We had met at the Texas Renaissance Festival near Houston in '01. We had recognized each other as having bonded in a previous life, and wanting to continue it, jumped right into a relationship. It seemed the right thing to do. We were now in our thirteenth year.

She filled my mind with her talents, and all the good things of just being with her. She was everything a man - or at least this man - could ever look for in a partner.

I finished my chores. Living on a mountain top required a certain bit of effort, but offered much more in rewards. We had built our place on rough terrain, which in the next few years would prove to be very much to our advantage. I walked to a point of rocks just a few yards from our house, one of my favorite places. I stepped out on the last boulder. The creek in the middle of the canyon sparkled like a crystal ribbon 600 feet below. Turning to the left the walls of the canyon fell away slightly. To the west, they rose higher as they blended into the front range of the Rockies.

To the east I could see the road into my place down below as it wound into the canyon. Things were peaceful and quite, for now. I remembered the feeling of being able to sort out things while standing there. I could stand there and almost see Laramie, Wyoming some 50 miles away. The world seemed so big. It always helped with your perspective. I remembered back on how all this had come to be. As usual, the old man had something to do with it. He was the one that found paradise.

Idaho

Damien drove the fifty miles or so from his cabin in the Idaho Mountains near Coeur d' Alene to the Spokane hospital. His Aunt Jean was close to death. She had sent for him last evening, but the spring snow storm had made the roads difficult. So he waited till this morning. His Aunt Jean was his only relative, having lost his parents at an early age. He couldn't really remember what had happened, he was only a toddler. He frowned. Snow was starting to pick up. He hoped he would be able to get back home this evening. He pulled off the Interstate and drove the few blocks to the hospital, parked his truck, and found his way inside. The lobby was full of patients and visitors. *Well, at least the health care business is booming* he thought. It seemed as if half the world was sick. What would happen if some kind of calamity was to strike? Without these hospitals, that half wouldn't make it.

He shook these negative thoughts from his head as he entered his aunt's room.

"Hi Auntie, how is my favorite girlfriend?"

"Oh, Damien, I'm so glad you could come. But you better not let Sandy hear that, she will be jealous. Did you leave her at home? I would have loved to see her, too."

"She had to work today. I probably won't be able to stay long, it is starting to snow again. The roads are pretty bad."

"Well come here and sit down. There is something I need to tell you. Actually, I should have told you a long time ago, but I just never quite found the right time."

"OK, you have my attention. Shoot."

"Well, when your parents were killed, I was living in St. Louis. I had not had much contact with my sister for a number of years. I had been in a bad marriage, and was quite self-absorbed. It was about six months after the accident before I finally received word of what had happened. I dropped everything and flew to Seattle. Finally, after several weeks of searching I found you in a foster home. The authorities gave me custody of you, and we have been family ever since."

"OK, Auntie, some of this is new and some of it I know."

"Well, what you don't know is, there was something else I haven't told you. When you were younger, it wasn't important. Later on it was so futile that I finally gave up the search."

"Gave up the search? Gave up the search for what, Aunt Jean?"

"Damien, you have an older brother somewhere. His name is Jeff. I searched for years, not telling you, not wanting you to have that disappointment."

He sat down hard. His head spun with that bit of knowledge. *Oh my God, a brother!*

"Aunt Jean, please tell me all you know, all you have found out. All my life, there were dreams of someone that played with me, someone who slept close to me. Just shadows of memories that I could never quite grasp and hang on to for long."

"OK, here it is. You were only two and a half, and he was twelve. After I found you, it took away from my time to search. When I did, I found that finally after being in a couple of foster homes he was with a family by the name of Bryan. It seemed that he didn't fit well with the family. When they attempted to adopt him they told him they would change his last name. He refused. They were living near Boise, Idaho. He insisted that he be able to keep the family name. When they persisted, he ran away. By this time he was a little over sixteen years old. The last thing I had heard was he was around Austin, Texas."

"Thank you, Auntie, for telling me this. So our family name was Bartlett, but you gave me your name."

"Yes, legally speaking. It was easier to adopt you. But anytime you want to take your name back I won't be offended, I promise!"

He thought for a minute. "No Auntie, you have been the only mother I really remember. I am proud to have your name, I would never change it!"

"It is also your mother's maiden name as well. I changed my name back after my divorce."

"That is even better!"

He leaned over her frail body and give her a soft hug and kissed her on her forehead.

"I love you, Auntie. Thank you for telling me this. I will continue the search for Jeff."

They talked for another hour. She had pictures of their family, pictures he had never seen. In the pictures one of them was of a young boy of ten or eleven. Holding in his arms, a baby. A look of wonder and adoration on the boys face. *My brother.* A whole new set of words in Damien's vocabulary. As he drove back with the snowflakes blowing across his windshield that evening, his thoughts ran wild. *Where are you Jeff? Do you remember me? Do you know I even exist?* He thought of the picture and the way the boy was looking at the baby. *Yeah, you remember!*

The snow was piling up as he pulled into the yard. He was happy to see lights on in the cabin, it meant Sandy was off work and home safe. He saw fourteen year old Russ loading the last load of firewood into the wood door on the side of the cabin for tonight's heat and hot water.

He shut off the truck and turned out the lights.

As he stepped out he yelled, "Hey Russ! Are the horses taken care of for the night?"

"Yeah, Dad. Is it ever going to stop snowing?"

"Yeah, about June." He laughed. It was a late spring it seemed.

As Russ and Damien entered the foyer where they kicked off boots and hung up coats, he could smell Sandy's spaghetti sauce and garlic bread. *Oh God, that smells good!* Cissy, their ten year old, was busy helping her mom, being the efficient little housekeeper she seemed to want to be. Cissy was named after an ancestor of Sandy's called Narcissa. She hated the name, and insisted on being called Cissy instead. Both the kids had been home schooled to the third grade, and even now they still got some homeschooling. They had been lucky enough to find a charter school that allowed them to do that, but it forced Sandy into working part time at an accounting firm in Coeur d' Alene.

Damien slipped up behind his lovely wife and kissed her on the side of the neck. She wiggled a bit and said, "Quit that, or the kids are going to have a late dinner. How is Aunt Jean? I would like to have been able to go with you. Darn life, it gets in the way of enjoyments sometimes."

"She is slipping fast. The doctors said it is just a matter of time. Something about heart valves, and she is too old and feeble. She could never stand the surgery. But, I have something to tell all of you and something to show you that you just won't believe. But dinner first."

Sandy's pasta sauce was always good, but tonight it was special. The family didn't talk much, just ate. Living an outdoor active life kept everyone hungry. No picky eaters here.

After dinner as was their custom each one picked up his serving utensils and washed and rinsed them and stacked them neatly in the drying rack. The table was cleaned and the kids went and got their schooling and computers, and came to the table to do homework. As they all sat down, Damien turned to Cissy and handed her one of the pictures, saying, "Cissy, check this out."

She looked and said, "Who is that, Dad?"

"That baby, my dear, is your own father. And the boy holding him is......Your Uncle Jeff, my older brother."

Damien thought the table was going to overturn. Everyone had to get a look at the picture. He went on to say, "The older man is my father, Nathan. The lady is my mother, Amanda."

The room was alive with questions. *Where did you get these? How long have you known? Where is Uncle Jeff now?*

Damien answered all of them except the whereabouts of his older brother. Damien's answer was, "We are going to take it as a family project to find him. Aunt Jean said his last known whereabouts was near Austin, Texas."

Immediately, Russ was on face book searching for a Jeff Bartlett. His quick answer was, "There must be a zillion Jeff Bartletts. But I will message all of them one at a time."

Damien thanked him for his zeal. As the conversation waned and everyone got into their studies, Damien switched on the evening news. Anderson Cooper was just breaking news. Terrorists had stolen two nuclear bombs, during a coup attempt in Russia. The theft was several days old. It was finally being released to the public. A world wide search was on. This was serious.

It wasn't long after September 11, 2001 that most of The Thinkers realized that an era was over. Let's face it, ideas change. We evolve. People don't want the same things that people 10 years, 20 years, 30 years ago wanted. It is inevitable, if you read your history books, that things change. We must all change with them. It seemed that the early 2000's seemed to the passerby to be a time of disunity - every man for himself. Service of almost any type became unheard of and communication became obsolete in the advent of the communication era.

Huge corporations would bail on their people, CEO's pulled outlandish salaries while labor suffered. It was a time when the rich were for the rich, and the public was clueless.

The war against Terrorism was waged around the world. The Old Man said "Terrorists are like fire ants. You can kill them out for a while, but when you go to attack others, they will come right back!"

But like all things after a few years, the stories became to unimportant for the media to follow and life balanced itself. The environment seemed to get most of the air time. The President had wanted to open up the arctic for oil drilling and also some places in the Colorado Rockies, but every freedom loving, left wing, outdoor loving Hippie, tree hugging liberal in the country got in his face about it. Of course, they still complained about the price of gasoline at the pump the next day. But the planet was doing some very erratic things. Temperatures were rising, storms got worse, friction on several of the large faults was building. It seemed that the planet was just poised in space, waiting for something to happen, something big. Evolution for the species was overdue.

My mountain retreat was taking shape. Great care was taken to make it as energy efficient as possible. We built battery banks, set up wind generators, solar panels and back up generators for emergency use. We built to utilize the sun, the wind, and the terrain. We used lots of stone and dead trees that had not fallen. We recycled everything twice. We developed ways of using magnified light, using crystals and fiber optics to grow our vegetables and fruits. Our natural spring provided us with all the water needed

to water our plants and animals and ourselves. We had found a source of big sheets of tempered glass for almost nothing. So we built lots of greenhouses and outbuildings, roofed with glass - this turned out to be very beneficial in the long winters in providing excellent solar heated shelters.

In season we hunted elk and deer and we were even forced at one point to kill a bear. We didn't want to, but he kinda forced the issue. We had quail and grouse and wild turkey. Life was good.

Those are the memories that fill my dreams now. I'm glad I have them. I can still see Nell, tending her plants in the nude, inside the steaming greenhouse. My favorite picture. I can see her turn and look and see me standing there watching. She would smile and accuse me of being a peeping Tom. Guilty as charged. I can remember those evenings beside the fireplace, on the soft skin that Mr. Bear and been so nice to donate, watching the snow fall in to darkness across the valley to the east, the lights of Fort Collins provided a glow in the low horizon beyond. Fort Collins, where have your lights gone?

But wait, I kinda got ahead of myself. You haven't met Nell, have you? After acquiring my mountain, I had to go back to Texas. It was after 9-11, and I need to settle my affairs. I had some money in a Credit Union from construction jobs I had worked. So here I am back near Houston again, and The Texas Renaissance Festival was in full swing. I had worked at it in the past and it was an exciting place for a young single man. Parties and pretty girls, and play acting. So I called an old friend and asked if he had a job for me. He did, so I worked the eight weekends of the show. The very first Sunday I went to one of the food shops to pick up a Steak on a Stake, and next door at the Muffalatta Shoppe was this really cute blonde girl. I smiled and tipped my hat. She curtsied, flashing a big smile, and some gorgeous cleavage. We each went our way.

After fair closed later that evening I heard there was to be a drum jam at Ed's place. With a somewhat limited social calender, I attended. Low and behold there was that cute blonde girl again. This time I walked right up and introduced myself.

"Hi, I'm Jeff," I blurted out.

"Hi I'm Nellia, better known as Nell," she smiled back.

"I saw you at the food booth earlier today," I added.

"I remember!"

We sat and talked for about a half hour. Someone had built a fire, and the drums had started. People had started to dance.

Nell stood and started to move her feet to the beat, then her hips and then her whole body. The thin light shift she was wearing was actually a sarong, and it didn't hide all her assets, but rather enhanced them. I sat entranced watching her. My heart beat so fast I could hardly breathe. The drums stopped, she walked over.

"Wanna go for a walk?"

We walked out to the narrow paved street called Renfaire Drive and strolled hand in hand in the bright moonlight. I told her about my place in Colorado, about how on the mountain you could see millions more stars than here, and how fresh the air was. She listened intently to every word.

The faire flew by. Within a week Nell and I had become inseparable, except during work hours. We became lovers and mates, and felt as if we had always been that way. The last weekend of the faire came and ended. I was packing to go back home to my mountain. I asked Nell, "Where are you going now?"

She smiled. "If someone would invite me, I would like to see a certain mountaintop in Colorado."

My knees buckled, I dropped to them in front of her.

"Oh, My! I was so afraid to ask, I was afraid you would say No! Yes, yes, I want you to go!"

I told her my place was not totally complete, that the next winter might be less than comfortable sometimes, but given another year it would be almost done.

She explained that if she was not with me, no place would be comfortable. We talked about our age differences. She was almost twenty, I was thirty two. She said that was perfect.

And that is the way it happened. She loved our mountaintop at first sight. When, one morning, feeling extremely playful, she pulled off all her clothes and ran nude out into the yard and lay down and made a snow angel, her nipples were standing straight up. She looked up and our neighbor James was standing there looking down at her.

He turned and said, "Uh, Jeff, I think we need an introduction."

I grinned. "Uh, James meet Nell!"

She squealed and jumped up totally red, and ran inside. I invited James inside. She had donned her robe by now. James has been in love with her ever since.

Sometime in 2010 I began to notice the news reels about what was going to happen in 2012. Movies were made about the catastrophes that were to occur on December 21, 2012. But no one seemed to know exactly what would happen. Conjectures were rampant. Technology had advanced by leaps and bounds. Your telephone was not only a telephone any longer, it was your personal computer and managed every phase of your life. One can only wonder what would be next, if we only knew then what we know now, what would come to pass in the next years.

I have become somewhat interested in politics in the past few years and even though my feelings were much toward the Democratic side, I considered myself a conservative. I was somewhat upset that the political party who call themselves conservative were so very non-conservative in their actions. As I said, I leaned a little toward the Democrats. But I considered them for the most to be weak, willy-nilly and tree huggers. Needless to say I did not enjoy listening to Democracy Now. I didn't like being called an Independent, because I always really despised anyone who just sat on the fence. The term Libertarian made me squirm as well. It was fast becoming a very difficult world to live in. There seem to be little to unify ourselves around. More focus was being given to whether two men could be married, or two women. I found the situation ridiculous. I had watched lots of marriages. The only thing that was important was the feeling of the people that were dedicating their lives to each other. Pieces of paper fall apart so easily, and ceremonies are meaningless. The only thing important was that feeling of completeness when you find that right person. Nothing else.

It was sometime in 2010 as well when some study was done and it was found that the U.S. was more divided than it had been any other time in history back to 1861. Wow, 1861! I thought we were better than that. We even had our first black President. Well, true he was not raised in the southern part of the United States or the north - he was born in Hawaii and spent his early years in Indonesia. He came from a poor background and he educated himself, had a beautiful wife and two lovely daughters. They were examples to all of us with their unity, their health, their energy.

But even with all that, the heavy stifling fog of prejudice hung over the country, making it blind to all the real dangers that are really lurking in the darkness. Makes one wonder what could happen to make things change.

In 2010 the Iraq war ended for the most part. But to my chagrin President Obama had sent 30,000 troops to Afghanistan. I was very disappointed. History had many points that no one could conquer these people, from Alexander the Great, to Kublai Khan, the British and the Russians had all failed. And to see our young men and women going there seems so pointless.

From time to time over the years I had received a letter or a phone call from the young man I had given the ride to Abilene. He had entered the Army after his father died and had done a tour in Iraq and was now on his way to Afghanistan. He had become a Ranger. His words were not encouraging, he did not feel that Iraq would survive after the U.S. pulled out. David had become a fantastic young man.

The theories about all the destruction that would happen in 2012 continued to get headlines. There were stories about planetary alignments that would shift the earth off its axis. For the most part I just ignored it. After all, the Y2K thing had proved to be a farce. Dooms-dayers had existed all throughout history, and I just expected more of the same.

Our place in the mountains was all complete now. We had most of the comforts that others in the cities had, and with a lot more space. Most afternoons and early evenings were spent with our horses and our dog, riding in the national forest behind our property. Almost every day we would see elk or deer, and an occasional bear. We enjoyed the fresh mountain air and the solitude and peacefulness of the forest. We raised most of our food - vegetables that is - and bought our meat from local ranchers whose herds roamed the the mountains and valleys and fed on the wild grasses.

Over the years several neighbors had moved near us, but not too near. For most part, they were like-minded people - interested in a self-sustaining low-impact life away from the cities. We would get together on occasion with potluck dinners, or to watch a movie, or just to talk. Often, the subject would change to wonderment on how fast our society was declining. How long would it be able to sustain itself? Sometimes the conversation will go on late into the evenings, planning what we could do if worse circumstances were to prevail. If we could've only known what was to happen in the very near future.

Every year it became more obvious that our climate was changing, and 2011 was no different. In the southwestern part of the United States very little rain had fallen during the last part of 2010, the drought continued into 2011. Texas seem to be the hardest hit, with little or no rainfall in the spring. In June a large wildfire broke out northwest of Houston, burning several homes and buildings. And this was just a start. There were many small grass fires. The fire departments were busy all summer. In late August a large wildfire broke out near Austin, burning many homes, devastating whole communities.

Federal help had to be brought in to bring it under control, but even before it was controlled, another large fire broke out near Houston near where the spring fire had burned.

The impact of these fires would be felt for years to come. Since no grasses had grown during the summer, and no hay had been grown, all the feed for cattle and horses had to be a trucked in. Prices skyrocketed, ranchers were forced to sell off their herds. It became so expensive that people would turn their horses loose because they couldn't feed them.

It was announced by the media that the price of beef would increase sharply for the next few years because ranchers herds had been so reduced. The worst of this was in Texas. But because feed had to be brought from all over the country to feed the Texas animals, it drove the prices up all over the place, even in Colorado. And even here, people started selling their horses, or giving them away. If they only knew.

In the past few years the BLM had been making major war on the Mustang herds in Nevada, Wyoming, Montana, and other places. The excuse was the herds were overgrazing the lands where they roamed, the truth was, the big ranchers wanted the Lands to graze their cattle. Laws were passed, legalizing slaughterhouses for horses, under protest of Mustang enthusiasts. Here again, if we could've only looked into the future.

Other events in 2011 that would reshape the future were the Arab Spring uprisings. It seemed to the observer that the whole world was on fire, and would surely burn up. It started with Tunisia, then spread to Egypt, and Bahrain, and Yemen. Then the people of Libya set out to overthrow Qaddafi, a process that would take thousands of lives in several months of hardship to accomplish, but would end in success. Late in the fall of 2011 we started hearing of protest in Syria that continued to escalate through the winter and into the spring of 2012.

My friend, David Suttle, was in his second tour of Afghanistan. His words painted a rather discouraging picture of that world. Graft among the countries leaders, drug production and addiction, the poppy was the national flower.

Our own military industrial machine was wasting millions of dollars on equipment that was being demolished for scrap and sold to Pakistan to made back into war machines. All the while, the U.S. and Pakistan continue to squabble over the border wars with Afghanistan.

The U.S. said their greatest fear was Pakistan's

nuclear arsenal and how safely it was protected.

There were also fears that Iran was building nuclear bombs, and Israel was talking of striking Iran. But all of you know this. You were there. I do hope you were paying attention, but I don't know if you were, I'm afraid a large part of the younger people were not.

The TV comedian Jay Leno often did a comedy sequence called Jaywalking. In it he would go out to public places and ask people the simplest questions about world leaders and events, sometimes showing them pictures. Some of the answers were so ridiculous, it was obvious people did not know what was going on around them. The only thing they seem to understand was entertainment, and fashion, and shopping, and everything else occurred outside of their world.

The world that would soon disappear before their very eyes.

I sit sometimes here in the mountains and

think of those events and replay them in my mind, still in disbelief that it could actually have happened. Tears come into my eyes, when I realize the number of friends and kin that I will never see again.

Chaos didn't happen though in 2012, life just went on same as ever. My own thoughts were that somehow Russia and Red china was somewhere back in the dark behind all this. Russia and China both sided with Iran, who was supplying Assaud in Syria. It just got more and more complex every year. I fully expected to see China start moving on other Southeast Asian nations, like Japan and the Philippines, or maybe Vietnam, and Thailand. And maybe Russia invading somewhere like the Ukraine, or Crimea. Something was bound to happen.

We almost had chaos in our world though. June 8th, 2012 a fire broke out in the mountains to our southeast. It burned thousands of acres, including a part of the Poudre River Canyon almost as far up as Rustic. It was horrifying to see these beautiful mountains burned and scarred that way. I couldn't help wonder if they would ever come back.

July 23, 2022

July in Colorado is a pleasant time and July 2022 was no different and toward the end is even more pleasant. The late afternoon usually gets abbreviated with a thirty to forty minute shower, which chases the heat away, and holds it at bay until the sun drops below one of the mountains to the west and it never gains it's strength back, leaving you with a sunny cool afternoon to do whatever is your pleasure. We had just finished one of those pleasures - riding our horses a few miles to the south to the top of Grey Rock and overlooking the Cache de Poudre River. We sat for a few minutes and smoked a couple hits of some fine Sensimilla and watched the late afternoon colors unfold. We made a small camp and spent the night.

We slept in the next morning, snuggling and making love until we realized that if we didn't get started we wouldn't make it back by dark. By the time we returned to our place at Fortress

Rock we had lost most of our light. We unsaddled and rubbed the horses down, fed them and went inside. Nell was fixing a bit of food, so I sat down and turned the TV on to CNN to find out what was happening in the outside world. I was not prepared for what I heard.

The first picture was that of a mushroom cloud, in all it's hideous glory, unfolding itself into the stratosphere some where over Africa. OMG. But wait, that wasn't enough. Here was another, somewhere near the first. The implications of one was limitless, but two? They're close to each other, what next?

Nell had heard my gasp and was looking over my shoulder, a look of disbelief on her face. All the while the anchor was describing what everyone thought to be accidents. The two bombs were being transported by a known radical terrorist group. It is unknown how or why they were detonated. They were about a hundred miles apart at the time some where in the Mali, Niger, Nigeria area.

My first thought was of family and friends, we went to our computers, and started leaving messages for those important to us. I knew this was going impact the U.S. I didn't know how yet, but some sense of foreboding came over me. I immediately placed some online orders for some things I had been putting off. I turned and asked Nell to order more seeds of various kinds. She nodded, and turned to her task. We spent the rest of the evening chatting with friends and discussing what impact this might cause in the U.S. One of my friends was in the Air Force and was involved in the weather sent me a message and said that I should pay close attention to storms coming off of Africa. This was Hurricane season. We had already had quite a bit of activity in the past few weeks. It was extremely hot in Texas and on the east coast, and The Weather Channel had made several references to the higher than usual water temperatures along the north of the Equator. We turned our computers off and sat down to talk. We discussed things we might order such light bulbs and other items we didn't keep in large supply. I made a mental list of ammunition reloading items and powder and lead, and went back and ordered everything that I couldn't pick up in Fort Collins.

Next morning we drove down to Fort Collins. We stopped in La Porte and had breakfast at Vern's and dropped off mail at the Post Office. All the talk was about yesterdays bombs and what was going to happen from the wildest conspiracy theories to some basic good ideas. I went to my favorite gun store and picked up several pounds of powder and was on my way out the door when I spotted a 1903 model 30-06 Springfield. It looked like it had just been taken out of cosmoline. I asked the guy how much he wanted.

"$350. Naw, you buy a lot of stuff, $300 for you."

"I'll take it," I answered. I already had one. These things were so simplistic and so accurate, and so enduring, I couldn't help it.

We went shopping. Nell bought some material, sewing thread, needles, buttons, things that could get scarce in a time of need. Next stop was Cost Co. We bought bandages, antiseptics, rubbing alcohol and aspirin, some other pain relievers, and other sundry items. By this time we decided to go have dinner before making the drive up the canyon.

We selected one the restaurants in the old town area and were in the process of devouring a really nice T-bone, when someone said, "Damn, I didn't think you guys ever came down off that mountain!"

"Depends on who think we might run into!"

I turned to see our buddy Dave. We had known Dave first in Texas, he traveled with renaissance festivals. Not that Dave was a hippie or anything like that. He wasn't. It's just he was a talented artistic woodworker, and the faires furnished him with an endless supply of girls. And Dave liked girls.

"What are you doing in Fort Collins, Dave?"

He came and hugged both of us.

"Well, the faire is over here in Colorado, and I wasn't sure what I was going to do for the next few weeks. Don't want to go to Minnesota this early. Thought I would come up and see if I could find you guys, and here you are."

"Well, lucky you, I guess. Did you bring your yurt?"

"I did. You have room for it?"

"Always."

We sat and finished dinner and talked about the events of the last few days. Dave shared some stories of life on the RenFaire circuit. We paid our bills, and made the long drive up the canyon. We arrived at the bottom of the hill, the last quarter mile to our cabin. I stopped and walked back and asked Dave to be sure to lock his hubs for the drive up. He had a small trailer, not to heavy, but our driveway required four wheel drive every trip. It was only a quarter-mile but it went from 6600 feet elevation to 7200 feet elevation in that short distance. He did and we all made it up the hill OK.

We welcomed him inside and told him he could set-up tomorrow just hang with us for the night. He thought that a good plan.

I turned on the TV and naturally enough every channel was buzzing about the bombs. Evidently the death toll was high in that part of the world, even as sparse as it was. Speculation was that radiation would kill thousands more. No one seemed to have any idea of the full extent of the damages so far. It had been a long day, so after unloading our purchases, we said our good nights, settled in for the night.

Nell and I took our showers and crawled into our king-sized bed. We had a window open, and as we lay for a while listening to the night sounds drifting in from outside, an occasional coyote, a nickering snort from the horses, night birds, we drifted off, cuddled in each others arms. We loved our home on the mountain.

Next morning I awoke to hear a conversation about what food is good for you and different ways to fix it, whatever that meant. I pulled my robe from a hook and donned it and made my way out to the kitchen slash living room slash movie theater slash office. We had built a round house out of cord-wood and masonry. We had built it with ten-foot high walls thirty-six foot in diameter, the center peak was at the fifteen foot mark, with a fireplace and kitchen built around it supporting the center. It was a sturdy home that was easy to heat and cool. It contained about all we need for our living, day to day.

I emerged from my peaceful sleep to a heated argument. Dave and Nell were discussing the wherewithal's of a proper breakfast. Dave, shirtless, his long hair worn loose and Vandyke beard, made an interesting picture wearing a pretty little yellow apron with frills. Nell, on the other hand, was wearing a little short dress, that ever time she stretched to reach something showed just a tiny bit of a very cute butt. As I entered they both turned.

"You guys sure aren't easy to sleep around," I yawned.

"Must not be too difficult. We have been up for two hours. The horses are fed and watered, and breakfast is ready," Nell retorted!

"Yeah, what she said!" Dave added.

I thought to ask what they had done the other hour, but decided to keep silent. I knew they had a little thing for each other bodies, but that was their business. Nell was devoted to me in every way. We had a good life together, but I was older than she, and she was a very sensual, amorous woman, and I was not going to stand in her way of a little fun now and again. She was always very discrete and it had never been more than an occasional happening. None of our neighbors and few of our friends knew about it.

I took my plate and moved to my chair, picking up the remote and flipping the TV on to The Weather Channel. Jim Cantore was standing on a beach somewhere, talking about a recent hurricane. But just as I tuned in, he started a conversation with someone in their studios about a storm just coming off the coast of Africa on the southern side of the Cape. He was saying that it looked to have real potential for development. This was Wednesday morning. On Thursday morning The Weather Channel stated that storm number one is live and well, and number two is just coming off lower Nigeria.

We spend the day walking in the National Forest, ending in late afternoon at the skinny little waterfall that dropped 75 feet into a pool that the water felt just a little short of being frozen. It was fed by a spring that came out of the ground not even a mile up the mountain. It didn't have time to even to be warmed by the hot July sun at all. We did as we normally did, pulled our clothes and shoes off our bodies made sweaty by hours of hiking at seven to eight thousand foot elevation. We simply ran across the knee deep pool about 30 feet across, stepped under the waterfall, screamed at the top of our lungs and ran back and jumped out before our feet and legs turned blue. Nell was like a vision to watch in the beautiful setting. Her beautiful nude body against the water and the rock was a sight to remember. The short quarter mile walk back to our house was just enough to get us warmed up again.

We sat outside on the rim of the Canyon in our sky chairs and passed a bowl around of good Colorado bud. Pink Floyd was playing in the background. *'How I wish, how I wish you were here......'.* Life was good!

Nell and I retired about 10 or so, leaving Dave drawing pictures of a woodworking project he had in mind. Sex with my girl was always a dream come true, tonight was no different. As we cuddled and basked in the afterglow I said,

"Well, did you and Dave have fun this morning?"

She cocked her head sideways and looked at me.

"Of course, I always have fun with Dave. Is it a problem?"

"How could it be a problem after the experience of a couple of minutes ago? No, darling, it could never be a problem as long as you love me and remain my best friend and partner!"

She wiggled closer and threw her leg over me, squeezing me with her entire body.

"Then it will never be a problem, 'cause that's not gonna change. You mean to much to me in a hundred different ways, and ---" she hesitated, "if it does get to be a problem, I will know, and it will stop. I don't need other guys. They're just fun sometimes."

I squeezed her and kissed her delicious lips and said, looking her in the eyes, "I Love You!"

I was a lucky guy.

Next morning I awoke a little earlier. I went out to the living room, leaving Nell snuggled into her pillow. Dave was asleep on the couch. I turned the TV on to The Weather Channel. Their studio was alive. The first storm had already reached category three status, number two was already at two, and another storm had formed and was exiting Africa as they spoke. Their experts were predicting the these storms to reach major proportions, their models were going crazy, but the first two appeared to be headed for the Gulf of Mexico at the moment. About that time, Dave piped up.

"Ah, weathermen. None of them know what they're doing."

Dave had always said that. He just didn't believe in weathermen. But just looking at their maps, it looked really bad.

About then, Nell came out of the bedroom

wiping her eyes sleepily, wearing her little nighty from last night. It did nothing but make everything look good, and hid nothing. I heard Dave, under his breathe mutter.

"Fuck."

I agreed.

"Nell, go put some clothes on, so we can think of something else," I asked softly.

She smiled, blew a kiss, and turned back into the bedroom. She appeared in a few minutes in a robe and house shoes, and her hair piled up on her head with a shower cap on her head.

"This better?" she smiled.

"Yeah, but even like that, you are still the cutest thing in the world."

"Thanks," she said and turned to the kitchen.

After breakfast, Nell changed into shorts and halter top. That was just too enticing, so I pulled Dave away. We climbed into my truck and went down to Cherokee Park Road to my UPS and mail box. We had ordered all our supplies from a couple of days ago for next day delivery. I checked my list and it seemed that everything had arrived. We stacked the truck full of boxes and strapped them in, and drove slowly back to the Fortress. I talked Dave into going for a ride with me so we saddled the horses and rode east along the canyon. Our place had about four neighbors up on the ridge where we lived. The first was the Roberts. Jim's dad had been a realtor in the area for years, and his great grandparents had settled this area in the 1870's. Jim was in the barn when we arrived. He came out to greet us.

"Hey, Jeff, where is that cute wife of yours? I would much rather be visited by her than you!" He grinned.

I turned to see a smiling face peering through the kitchen window.

"Marion!" I hollered "Jim's flirting with Nell again, and she isn't even here!"

I turned to Jim. "Jim, meet Dave. He is a friend of mine visiting."

Marion's answer came through the window, "I don't blame him, I'm in love with her too!"

"Morning, Dave. Lite and let your horse rest."

"I'll be happy to do just that, but it isn't for my horses benefit. I am not used to this kind of transportation!"

We dismounted, tied the horses to a hitching post convenient to the deck.

Almost everyone had the hitching post. We all visited by horseback a lot up here. It was almost all Red Feathers National Forest, with few fences. A horseman's paradise.

I asked Jim if he had been watching the news, and what his thoughts were.

"Scares me to death, Jeff!" was his answer. "Of all the strange and terrifying events of the last couple of decades, this is the strangest and most terrifying. These two storms will wipe out all the Caribbean Islands at their present strength."

"There are three now," I added.
"Jeez, I didn't catch the last one."

We sat and visited for a half hour. He and Dave drank a cup of coffee. After a short while I excused us and said I wanted to show Dave around some more.

"Hey, give me a minute and I'll saddle up and tag along, if it's ok!"

"Sure, love to have you ride with us."

The next visit was to Mike McCullom and his wife Shelly. Mike was a distant cousin of Nell's, a hunter and outdoors-man. We had FaceBooked for a few years, and I finally kept showing him elk and deer pictures until he couldn't stand it anymore and sold their home in Wisconsin and bought a place up near us. As we arrived, his kids came running out, yelling, "Hey, Uncle Jeff!" Technically, I wasn't their Uncle, but I wore the badge with pride.

We visited with Mike and the kids for a while. Shelly had gone into Fort Collins. We were about to leave when Shelly topped the hill from the canyon below. The Jeep Cherokee she was driving looked like the it was on the Baja run.

Mike said, "Damn, wonder what crawled under her saddle?"

She slid to a stop, jumped out and said, "Jeff, Jim! I am so glad you are here. There is a panic in town. The stores are all being mobbed, all kind of conspiracy theories going round. I got out of there as quick as I could!"

We all looked at each other. *What the fuck!?* The U.S. is not in immediate danger yet and everyone was going nuts. We decided to cut our visit short. Mike said he would go talk to our other three neighbors on the mountain and get back with me later in the evening. Dave and Jim and I mounted up and loped back to the house. Jim dropped off at his driveway, waving bye as he did. We unsaddled and put the horses away.

As we entered Nell was sitting on the couch kinda curled up in a ball, watching the big screen as images flashed across it. Riots in cities on the east coast, and Southeastern U.S. Then, the first storm, a satellite view. It was a cat 5, it's third day of life. Number two was cat 4, and the little storm that had just come off this morning was already at hurricane level. Holy crap, they were lined up in a straight line more or less. But they didn't look like three storms, they looked like one long storm with three eyes. An evil three-eyed dragon crossing the Atlantic, headed for us.

I looked at Nell and Dave.

"Well, let's don't get too excited. Big storms have been born out there and died out there."

But in my heart of hearts I thought *Those poor people in the Islands*.

"Well, I think we should enjoy the evening. Get our mind off it. Check back in the morning, then maybe make some plans."

All agreed. Nell had taken some steaks out of the freezer for dinner. About that time the voice of Jim our neighbor came over our CB radio base station.

"Hey, Jeff! We had some steaks that crawled out of the freezer and committed suicide. Can we bring them over and have a cremation service?"

I keyed the mike and answered, "Jim, the charcoals are warming up."

The answer was, "Be there in five."

By the time we got the steaks and everything out to the cooker and had started the setting up Jim and Marion pulled up on their ATV. Dave took charge of the grilling, the girls,after some girl conversation, were putting salads and sides together. Jim came over and handed me a beautiful hand blown pipe. "Here, try some of this. It is one of my hybrids. It is all thought provoking, no body downing at all. When it goes away, you won't notice any difference at all."

I took a hit on the pipe. Within seconds, an extreme awareness of my surroundings took over my thoughts. I turned to Jim and gave him a thumbs up. I walked out to the end of my deck overlooking the creek 600 feet below. I looked across at the faces on the other cliff face across the canyon. The faces etched in the rocks by the hands of time and wind and erosion seemed to change as the shadows moved with the fading light. As the sun was dropping behind the mountains to the west, a goldie hung almost motionless, fifty or sixty yards out in front of me. As I watched, the stereo system came on behind me. John Fogerty's voice carried out on the afternoon breeze '*Long as I remember.....*'

I think that is the first time I started to worry about my paradise a bit.

I started to think about the Old Man again. He had always said that some thing like this would happen eventually. He said the way our population was exploding, the vast gap in wealth distribution, would be major causes. He said our small planet couldn't handle that much crowding, with such poorly managed governments. Also, those downtrodden people of third world countries will turn to hate to try to rectify their situations. Their mainstay and driving force will turn to religion, religion that by it's on nature will be come extremist. It will never help them out of their situation, but it can and will play havoc on everyone else, and even themselves.

The Old Man had been a soldier in the Vietnam War of the 1960's. He spoke little of his experiences, but when he did, it was most usually to illustrate the behavior of the human species when placed in unfortunate and traumatic circumstances. I never heard him speak of his education, but most everything he said seemed to have wisdom in it.

I was jarred back to reality with a call.

"Steaks are done!"

Accompanied by the sounds of the Moody Blues' *Knights in White Satin,* I walked back and pick up a plate and scooped up some salad in a bowl, a scoop of mashed potatoes and my chunk of T-Bone, and poured brown gravy liberally over both them. I found me a seat by my favorite girl. She gave me a soft kiss and rubbed her hair on my shoulder. It always made me purr.

Idaho

Damien and Russ had just finished welding the last piece on the big grid for the wind turbines. The contract had been a fat and juicy one, but more than that, it was helping create something green for energy production. Damien had become involved with this work through Russ. Russ had gone to tech college in Spokane and had met people in the new green energy field that was getting a large amount of attention from everywhere except Washington, D.C.

Damien thought Russ was a prodigy of sorts. He had built a turbo generator himself and had installed it in the creek that ran near his cabin. And when Russ met Misty, and fell in love, he and Russ built them a cabin near his own. Cissy, now seventeen, was graduating from high school next year. Damien considered himself a lucky man. As Russ eased the big one ton dually, with it big welder and tanks, down off the mountain, Damien's thoughts were of the future. He still thought of his brother. He had not given up hope of finding him. But today life was good. He worked with his son, his family was close. He was forty three years old, Sandy was forty one. She had done extra schooling and now had her own business. She did the taxes for his and Russ' company as well.

"Dad, I forgot to tell you, I found some new candidates for the Uncle Jeff search. I sent a message to two of them this morning and will do the other one tonight after dinner."

"What do you think the chances are?" Damien asked.

"Well, the first two are in Texas. One in Austin, the other in Houston. They looked somewhat like he could look, I suppose. The third one is from some place in northern Colorado, a town called Fort Collins, I believe. His picture wasn't too clear. I will send it to you this evening and let you look at it."

A little over an hour later, they drove up the driveway to the two cabins. As the approached,

Russ said, "Crap, looks like we are having a party."

"Hmm, looks like!"

A couple or three cars and trucks Damien recognized as neighbors were parked off to the side. Ribbons were strung on ropes between the trees across the decks, smoke was drifting from the big barbecue pit on the deck. As Russ shut off the diesel, music was playing. Looked like a celebration of sorts. Sandy and Misty came running down to greet them with hugs and kisses.

" Congratulations. You guys go get a shower, you stink."

"Evidently we don't stink to bad to create a party," Russ said.

Misty giggled and wiggled her twenty year old frame. "You never smell too bad for me." Sandy looked at him and made a face.

He and Russ took a hurried shower and put on clean clothes and returned to their guests. They were greeted with several bowls of good Washington homegrown and soon were deep in conversations about new technology for energy and growing gardens hydroponically. Several their neighbors had green houses already. Soon the steaks were done and it was time to sit and visit. These people over the years had become Damien's family, a family he had never had. They had become especially important after his Aunt Jean had passed almost six years ago. Now, his family, with Misty newly added and his neighbors, he was almost content with his life.

The party broke up about ten. Goodbyes were said. Cissy wanted to go down to Coeur d' Alene with a friend and spend the night. Damien told her OK, but call in the morning, he would pick her up.

As the last car pulled away, Sandy and Damien stood watching the tail lights fade away through the trees, exploding occasionally when brakes were applied. They both looked up at the sky, just in time to catch a falling star. Sandy sighed.

"Such a beautiful peaceful night, Damien. Makes you think that all is well in the world."
 It was July 23, 2022!

Next morning Damien woke late. He walked out in his robe and stood talking to his horse Ben. Ben was wise in the ways of humans. You could tell all your troubles to Ben and he would sort it all out for you. As he was thanking Ben for his help, Sandy yelled out the door.

"Damien, come quickly!" Her voice had a tone of urgency to it.

Damien turned and hurried back. As he entered the TV was on CNN. Wolf Blitzer was explaining as two mushroom clouds filled the screen. Some where in western Africa, for some reason, two nuclear bombs had been exploded. No one was sure why. Wolf had a panel of experts giving their opinions, but it was useless prattle. The damage had been done. About then,

Russ and Misty burst through the door.

"Dad! Have you seen....," His voice trailed off.
"What is going to happen now?"

"Don't know, Russ. But I have a bad feeling about this. We should make ourselves prepared in case there are more of these, and they have some in this country. People have wondered for a long time if they could get one into the port at Seattle."

ଊ

After dinner we turned the TV on for a few minutes. Things were really beginning to look very bad. We were just turning it off when Mike and Shelly and Dan Hughes and his girl Kathy and George Hampton and Marie arrived. We welcomed them, introduced every one to Dave, and found places on the deck for everyone to sit. The talk was all about the storms and rioting. Everyone had an opinion of what we should do or not do. I mostly just listened. I had tried to make sure I had everything I needed on hand. I also felt it was too soon to know for sure what effect all this was going to have on me. The Old Man had always told me, and it had rubbed off on me, that you don't make a decision until you get all the facts. The facts weren't in yet.

After several bowls of good Colorado bud were passed, the conversations subsided. I took this opportunity to speak.

I was aware of Nell and Marion sitting off to themselves, talking quietly. Nell was stroking Marion's hair. They seem to be developing a really close relationship. That was good. In times like these, friends are a comfort.

"I hope you guys have gathered stores of staples and other thing you need in case the effects of this reaches us. Hopefully it won't. Also, we should keep our CB radios turned on all the time, so we can stay in touch with each other. We still have cell phones, but that technology still is a bit flimsy at best, and we shouldn't rely on it. A slight overload on any towers bandwidth and it's useless."

At that point everyone was thinking of warm beds, and after many hugs and reassurances that every thing was alright, all left and we were alone again.

Next morning Dave approached me.

"Jeff, you mentioned staples last night. How about yourself?"

I looked at him. "Dave, I'm going to show you something, but you must promise to never tell anyone about it. Promise!"

"Of course," he said.

I told him to follow me, and we went to the west side of the property to the tack rooms built up against the bank of the hill. I unlocked the door and went inside. We walked to the back side of the room. I took hold of a harness peg and lifted it, as I did a door opened out towards me. I swung it open, all the harness and tack still hung on it, behind it was another door. I opened it, and when I did a blast of frosty air blew into our faces. Dave stepped back for a moment. We stepped inside and I hit the light switch. Shelves of packaged meats, fish, frozen fruit and vegetables. Some blocks of ice sat in the corner.

Dave said, "Wow, how does this work?"

I answered, "It works on the same system as an RV refrigerator, just bigger. It takes forever to cool down and get this cold, but it is well insulated, and as long as it is not used often and kept closed it's perfect."

We stepped out and closed it all back up. The next door worked the same way, except is was at about forty degrees, it had containers of wheat, oats, barley, different kinds of dried beans, etc. etc. It was kept very dry. It also had shelves of canned jars of fruit, vegetables, juices, soups along with preserves, jellies, and jams.

We closed it all up and secured it. Dave slapped me on the back.

"I'm impressed! You really have thought of everything."

I grinned. "I can't take credit for everything. There was an old man that told me how to do a lot of this stuff."

We were on our way back to the house when Dave pointed out the tiny block building between the greenhouse and the house, asking, "What's that?"

"That's our furnace and water heater. It heats our house and green house and supplies all our hot water needs. It is virtually smokeless. It has a catalytic converter that burns most of it's ash. Burns about anything, too. You can buy them anywhere now, but we built this one."

As we sat down to breakfast I could hear a truck coming up the grade. It wasn't a new vehicle. I listened carefully asI heard it hit the top of the hill and turn our direction. I walked out on the deck and looked eastward, as I did an old Dodge Power Wagon pulling an even older trailer appeared through the trees. *Oh My God, it was the Old Man!* I raced back to the kitchen.

"Nell, It's the Old Man!"

She squealed and came running.

"Dave, you are in for a treat!" I said as I ran back out the door. He followed. By then the old truck had stopped and Nell was hugging the old man that just emerged. I was next and gave my very best bear hug.

"Pop," I said, " I would like for you to meet a good friend of mine. This is Dave."

The Old Man stuck out his big paw, saying, "My name is Chris. I guess he has smoked too much of this mountain weed he grows and has forgotten."

I told him that I had not forgotten, and he didn't have to keep embarrassing me in front of my friends. He just snorted and turned to Dave and told him he was glad to meet him and looked forward to getting acquainted. Dave nodded likewise.

I looked at the Old Man. He must be near about eighty by now, but he still had the air of a imposing person about him, a self assuredness that was comforting. He looked back at me and asked, "You have room for one more here?"

My answer, "Mia Casa, su casa. Always!"

I invited him to sit and Nell broke another couple of eggs and we sat down and finished our morning meal. After we finished I switched on the TV. I almost wished I hadn't. The picture before us couldn't have been thought up by one of Hollywood's finest. The storms were off the chart. Number One had already passed the Leeward Islands, although you really couldn't tell much. It seemed like the whole Atlantic Ocean was one big storm. Number One seemed to be headed right for Cuba, Number Two was bearing just a bit north toward Florida. All cities from Miami to South Carolina were under emergency evacuation. Number Three still hadn't made it's choice clear yet, but it still appeared to be heading kinda behind Number Two. This seemed rather unusual, yet there was nothing usual about any of this. Number Three was cat 5. The other two were, well, they were making up new numbers for them. The U.S. had granted Cuba right to evacuate as many as possible to the U.S. Several South American Countries had followed suit. Planes had been dispatched to fly through the storms. Two never returned. Barometric pressure, where it could be measured, had never been this low. All they could do was watch. Another day or two and, well, no one knew what to expect.

The Old Man moved his chair back from the table. He wiped his mouth and grey beard with a napkin.

He said, "Jeff, I think you should establish you a perimeter. Fortify yourself somewhat. I believe it is better to be prepared. You can always un-prepare if I'm wrong."

I replied, "Do you think it is going to come to that?"

"I just came from down in the San Luis Valley. I had to skirt Denver and Colorado Springs and every place else with any population. There are mobs of armed people everywhere. Yes, I'm afraid it might."

He added, "Is James still up here? How many others that you can trust?"

"Four families for sure, maybe some more over in the valley."

"We should have a meeting really soon."

We spent the rest of the day making plans, calling people near about us, as well as people elsewhere, and trying collect as much intel as possible. Dave found a place near the compound to set-up his Yurt. By evening his house was all cozy. The old man remarked upon entering it and looking around.

"I like this. Wish I had one, better than hauling that ratchity old trailer around. Hmm, too late now, done got too old!"

Old Chris had poured a ton of resources as well as skill, foresight, and motivation into Fortress Rock, as we liked to call it. I had thought of Robbers Roost when we first thought of naming it. But the real Robbers Roost lay about twenty miles to the North of us, at the border. It had been the hideout of Jack Slade, outlaw gang in the late 1800's. He would rob the stagecoaches at Owl Canyon, and also coming up the long hill out of Wyoming to the Colorado border while they were slowed down pulling the hills. His wife, Virginia Dale, had the stage stop just south of the state line, so he knew when the stages were coming through and what they were carrying. I wondered what these hills were about to experience again!

The next morning the news was being reported from location mostly in the western and central U.S. Nothing was coming off the east coast. Cuba had been dead since last evening. No reports from there. Houston, New Orleans, and all the other cities along the gulf coast were heading inland. Great long lines of traffic were shown at standstills for hundreds of miles. The east coast was doing the same thing, but they all had waited too long. Military jets flying high filmed pictures of one giant storm with three eyes. One in the Gulf of Mexico, one headed straight for Jacksonville, Florida, and the third headed somewhere between Washington, D.C. and New York City. But all the eastern seaboard was awash. Even now, the eyes were two hundred miles off shore, but cat three and four winds were onshore from Boston to the border with Mexico at Brownsville, Texas. *God help us all*. We turned the TV off and turned to look at each other. Who could have imagined this? A nightmare that could not have been made up even in a fright movie.

The Old Man sighed. "We can only guess what it will be once this is over. Millions will probably die. I believe it will be pretty much impossible to get fuel, and I guess a huge part of the grid will be down. I'm sure what most of what we take for granted will be lost."

By noon most of our neighbors had gathered. About ten families that I knew well, two or three others that I didn't know so well. I stood up to speak.

"Neighbors, friends, I am not going to waste our time talking about what has just happened or is going to happen in the coming days. We have developed some plans for our security and preservation. We think things will get chaotic. I hope we are wrong, but I would rather be wrong in this case, than unprepared."

Some guy, one of the ones I didn't know, pops up with, " Hey, who put you in charge, anyway?"

I asked, "What's your name, sir?"

"Mickey Grant," he answered.

"Well, Mr. Grant, no one has put me in charge. As yet, I am simply explaining what we are going to do. You are most welcome to do as you please, or go as you please. But in our boundaries, this what is going to be. If you choose to join us, then you will follow our rules. If you can't see your way to do that, then you won't be welcome. For the most part, rules are going to disappear for a while. But society can't exist without them. We will have them here. Any questions?"

Mike stepped forward. "I agree with Jeff. I

don't think it is a matter of who is in charge, at least at the moment. We all saw the news this morning. We need a plan, and we need organization. We must start with what we have!"

I interjected. "I don't know how many of you are ex-military, but I would like to introduce some of you to Chris. I have known Chris for about thirty years. He is a combat vet of the Vietnam War. He is going to want to get as many of you together as have military experience. Chris?"

The Old Man stood up. "Some of you know me, the others might call themselves lucky." He smiled. "I have been expecting something to happen for years. I had almost thought I was going to go to my resting place without being here for it. But ladies and gentlemen, I could never have dreamed of something like this. I believe we are going to be in for a tough time of it. Folks, the very nature of man is shown when something disrupts his day to day life he gets upset. That varies according to the character of the man. Some rise above it, some sink to the depths of deprivation. I watched people in Vietnam die and be mistreated by their own blood. The same thing happened in our own Civil War. We would be fools to think it couldn't happen to us, and it may very well happen, with such a catastrophe as we see unfolding."

The talks went on into the late afternoon. Discussions were held over proper security over food stuffs and home security. Plans were laid for a roving patrol to be set up, in case of danger. They would be a ranger force to go immediately to that home or ranch.

We all had citizen band radios and walkie-talkies. Codes were established so that anyone listening would not immediately know what was being discussed.

We all felt that we should collect all the horses and livestock and try to confine them to a secure place, especially at night.

Check points were set up on the roads and trails, and sentries posted on some of the rock towers, where one could see for miles. By then end of the day it appeared we were becoming a focused and organized group. Our trial by fire was yet to come.

I sat on the deck resting a few minutes, when Nell approached.

"Jeff, the internet came on for a few minutes. We got a message from a Russ Bradley. He wanted to know if you were the Jeff Bartlett from the Austin area. I tried to answer, but my reply wouldn't send."

"I'm not sure Nell. The name doesn't ring a bell. My mom's maiden name was Bradley. Other than that I have no clue."

Our evening meal was consumed on the deck I asked the Old Man, "Chris, do we really shoot people that come up here, and how do we know if it is necessary? How do we tell if they are friend or foe, don't we at least warn them?"

"You will know, and yes we will warn them. Tomorrow I am having some of the teenage boys make signs and post them at strategic places, both on the hill and creek and south of us down in the meadows. We have about forty-eight hours, maybe, before the shit hits the fan I calculate."

After dinner, we went in and turned on the TV. There wasn't much news. The storms were all onshore, cities everywhere, devastated. The storms were still cat 5 and above and miles inland. They didn't seem to be dying out like hurricanes normally did after coming ashore.

Sleep didn't come easy that night. I had friends and relatives, so did Nell, all in harms way. I knew lots of people must have died in the last few days. Nell and I lay with our arms around each other. Words weren't necessary. I awoke the next morning to find it raining. Raining hard actually. It rained all day, and it was almost tropical. It was a strange feeling, in the foothills of the Rockies. Wave after wave of thunderstorms passed over us all day, then two days. Then it was over. Our satellite TV didn't work for those two days. Then morning came and the feed returned. Most of it was being broadcast from the west coast. A satellite picture from one of the space stations looked down on a United States of America, about three-fourths of it's normal size. The news anchor spoke in a somber tone, trying to describe the pictures flying by of great cities laying in waste. Cities that simply weren't there anymore. Miami, Florida simply didn't exist, nor for that matter, any other cities in Florida. They just weren't there anymore. New York City lay in ruins. Washington D.C., The White House, The Capitol Building, all gone. Water extended to the foot of the Alleghenies, then covered most of Georgia, Alabama, Mississippi, Louisiana and a large portion of Texas. They said a hundred foot tidal wave had hit downtown Houston. The water in the mighty Mississippi was running upstream all the way to Keokuk, Iowa. I got up and went outside and leaned on the deck rail, over looking the Canyon. I just began to sob. My heart felt like it weighed a hundred pounds. Will we ever know how many souls perished? I felt soft arms around my waist. I turned and looked at eyes full of tears.

I hugged her. "We don't have time for this, we have work to do!"

She nodded. We turned and went back inside. Dave and the Old Man were wiping there own eyes.

We knew now that what we had expected had turned out to be worse than we had even dreamed. At that time we didn't know that the worst really wasn't over.

Chris, as I am going to call him now that he is present, gathered four or five teenage boys from the neighborhood and spent the next two day making signs and posting them in strategic spots about a quarter mile or so around the upper part of the hill we sat on. About fifty feet from every sign they placed a metal fifty-five gallon drum and painted them red with a black circle in its side about sixteen inches in diameter. They put several large rocks in each barrel so that it wouldn't tip over easy. Every trail was posted in this manner from every direction. Every sign and barrel was visible from at least two lookout towers. The procedure was to observe anyone coming toward us, the sign would warn them. If they chose not to heed the warning, one of the sentries would fire one round into that barrel. If they proceeded anyway, they would be fired upon in earnest.

WARNING!

FROM THIS POINT FORWARD YOU ARE BEING OBSERVED THROUGH THE SCOPE OF A HIG POWERED RIFLE. IF YOU WOULD LIKE TO ENTER, SEND NO MORE THAN TWO UNARMED.

IF YOU CHOOSE TO IGNORE THIS, IT WILL BE CONSIDERED AN ACT OF AGRESSION AND DEADLY FORCE WILL BE USED.

Later that afternoon James and Mike and myself, walked to the rock towers, climbed to the top and scanned the areas in our sections.

We wanted to make sure that we didn't leave any hidden paths into us. We also fired on the barrels. In most cases we could hear the impact as the bullets hit the barrels. The old man's idea was good.

We still didn't know if all this would be needed, but it was better to be prepared. Our TV feeds became more and more sporadic. We couldn't seem to get local news at all for some reason. We needed to know what was going on in Fort Collins and Denver. We decided a scouting party was necessary. We gathered three of our neighbors and Mike and James. We loaded into my Dodge Ram. Dave stayed home, Shelly and Marion came up and stayed with Nell. We armed ourselves with sidearms, but no rifles. We had walkie-talkies and a CB radio.

We drove cautiously down the gravel road leading out of Cherokee Park to US 287. There was no traffic. We stopped at the Livermore store, but it was closed. Mr. Broyles, the owner, recognized me and James and came out with his shotgun cradled in the bend of his arm.

"Morning, Jeff. Nice weather we are having!"

"Yes sir," I answered, "how are you fairing, sir?"

He went on to say that he had closed the store during the rain. He said he had seen several loads of men in cars driving up and down the highway, as of yet he had not had any trouble.

He also said that there had been a number of killings in La Porte and Fort Collins. This made us a bit nervous to say the least. After telling Mr. Broyles if things got dangerous, he would be welcome with us and try to bring as many stores as he could. He thanked us and we continued on our journey.

Down about haystack rock - so named because the ranchers would pile hay around it and sell it to the army back in the nineteenth century, scamming the army quartermasters - a semi-trailer lay on it's side, it's tires had been shot out. The big yellow McDonald's sign on the side explained why. Down around the corner, we pulled into Ted's Place. The windows were all broken out, the ice freezers dumped. In an old car sat two guys next to what had been the gas pumps, now destroyed. We drove on past Jim Bonners' place. No one seemed to be around, no vehicles visible.

As we drove into La Porte, little curses of disbelief escaped the lips of my passengers. The scene was like one of the disaster movies. Everything was wrecked. The people looked haggard and scared. I pulled up beside two women standing in the middle of the intersection. The signal light was dead. I asked one of them if she knew what was going on in Fort Collins.

Her answer was, "It's living hell! People are killing each other over scraps of food. There is no water or electricity anywhere. Cars won't run cause they can't gas anymore. Can you help us?"

I shook my head. "I'm sorry ma'am, we can't. It's bad everywhere."

She answered, "Please, we will do anything you boys want. We'll show you a really good time."

I shook my head, "I am sorry ma'am."

As I drove away, I caught sight of James handing two Cliff bars out the windows to them.

As we were just exiting La Porte, two men stepped into the road, with shotguns. I stopped about twenty-five yards short of them. I told Mike, in the passenger seat, to step out and talk to them, but stay behind the door.

He stepped out asking, "Hey guys, what's going on?"

One of them, a seedy looking guy in filthy cameo pants and a black muscle shirt with no muscles under it answered.

"How cum you guys got gas to ride around n' nobody else does?"

As he said this, he kept swingin' his shotgun up and down.

Mike answered, "We just haven't been going anywhere to run out yet."

The other man, younger and just as seedy as the first, pipes up. "Well, maybe you should share."

As he said this he stepped forward and started to raise his shot gun. Meanwhile I slipped my forty-four Mag revolver out of its holster and laid it across the side mirror, saying, "Gentlemen, lower those shotguns, or I am going to shoot you. This a forty-four magnum. Anywhere I hit you, you're probably dead."

I saw hesitation. The bigger guy, the first one's shot gun was low. The other one was still up. I took aim.

"Little man, you will be the first to go. Your gun is still up. Get it down now, and both of you turn around now, and start walking away. Don't stop for at least fifty yards. If you stop or turn back, I will shoot you. Do it, now!"

For a moment, I didn't think it was going to work. Then the big guy said something to the other. They lowered the guns and started to walk away. I waited until they were about seventy five yards away, and quickly made a u-turn and drove away. I turned to Mike.

"Well, I guess that answers our question. I didn't really need anything from town, did you?"

His only answer was, "Whew!"

We drove back up the hill. On arrival Chris asked what it was like. I said, "Imagine bad, then multiply it by ten!"

I looked around and asked Dave, "Where's Nell?"

He answered that Nell and Marion had

saddled up one of the horses and had gone to the waterfall. Oh Crap. I told everyone I was going to get them. I jumped on my dirt bike and headed off to retrieve the girls. It just wasn't safe for them to be alone.

I parked about a hundred yards before the falls it was pretty rough to get in there on a bike. I walked over the hill into the little narrow canyon that sheltered the pretty waterfall. I could hear the running water. I climbed around the last rock and there, in a patch of grass on a sunlit spot on a blanket, was the most beautiful sight any man could ever have happened upon.

Marion and Nell lay nude on the blanket, Marion on her back and Nell laying half draped over her. They were kissing softly, their arms around each other. Marion was stroking Nell's long blond hair, their breasts pressed against each other. It was an enchanting picture. Oh crap. I slowly backed back around the boulder, and walked back twenty yards or so.

I yelled, "Nell, Marion, are you there? Are you

decent? I'm coming up!"

"Hang on a sec, we are getting dressed!"

A couple of minutes past. "Come on, all clear!"

I walked back up and said, "Sorry to interrupt you, but we just got back from town. It's not really safe anymore to come down here unarmed or alone."

I went on to tell them of our trip, giving all the details. I saddled the horse and led it down to the trail and mounted my bike. After helping them mount, I couldn't help looking at them on the horse. Nell sat up front and Marion tight behind her, with her arms around Nell's waist. Lucky women!

The next few days went by uneventfully. We spent time preparing defense scenarios. On mid-morning on the third day we heard several shots coming from the valley to the north.

Mike, James and I jumped into the Dodge and headed down the steep hill as fast as we could go. As we came out of the valley we saw three or four men behind an old eighties model Lincoln. They were firing at the Nichols house. We stopped, and I leveled my .06 at the man on the left, and squeezed off a round. He spun backwards and fell. About that time Mikes' deer rifle barked and the second guy fell back into the car he was beside. The other two threw up their hands and dropped their weapons. We cautiously stepped out of the truck and walked toward them.

I yelled, "You move, you're dead!"

At that moment Dan Nichols came out the door. He walked towards us and as he reached us he turned and raised a nine mm automatic and shot one of the guys right between the eyes.

He turned and looked at me, his eyes full of anger.

"He shot Billie!"

Billie was Dan's wife. I asked what her condition was, he said he wasn't sure. he was just trying to keep these guys back and couldn't tend her. His daughters were tending their mom. I told James to get some zip ties out of my toolbox and restrain the last guy standing. I went inside to find Billie on the floor. Blood was trickling from a wound in her right side. I asked her if it was OK if i opened her shirt, she nodded. I found the wound, it would be OK. It went through the fleshy part of her side and out clean through, we need to get her to our place, so the girls could take care of her.

I turned to Dan. "Hook onto your RV trailer and come to the bottom of the hill. We will get a couple of four wheel drives and pull you up. You can't stay here."

He nodded.

I went back out front. Two of the men were

dead, including the one Dan shot. The one had a nasty wound in his shoulder, but he would live, barring complications. I turned to the other sitting against the old sedan, his hands secured behind his back.

"Who are you, where you from? What are you doing over here?"

He said, "Name's Ronnie. We're from over near Greeley. There's no food. We just wanted something to eat!"

"Yeah, so you shoot a woman?"

"Rod did that. I didn't want him to shoot. He's kinda a hothead. The man told us to leave. Rod got mad."

"You should have left."

Ronnie just kinda looked down.

By this time a couple of truck loads of

neighbors had showed up. People were talking hanging, and shooting.

I stepped up and said, "We are not going to do this. None of you know right now if you were as desperate as these people are what you might do yourselves."

I related about our trip to La Porte a few days earlier, ending with, "I think most of you have RV's or something. I think all of you should load up your stores and come up on the mountain. It isn't going to be safe down here. There is a bunch of National Forest, and I don't think anyone is going to get after you for squatting."

By the time I returned home, the neighbors had Billie comfortable on a cot in our living room. All the women were tending her, her wound had been cleaned and dressed. We were in luck. Two of our neighbor women were nurses - Dakota, and another girl named Diana. I felt much better about this.

By dark we had six motor homes and travel trailers parked in a semi circle around in the trees at the edge of our compound. The owners were making trips back to their homes and bringing up food stuffs and other important items. Johnny Mann down the road had a military six-by that he used to tow the big campers up our hill. I thought to myself *This is probably going to be an important piece of equipment to have on hand*. A couple of years ago I had installed an underground five hundred gallon tank. I kept about a hundred gallons of diesel fuel in it and refueled my truck out of it, always going back and refilling. I now had it almost full. It would last us for a while.

As the sun was sitting behind the foothills above Red Feather Lakes I walked out on the deck overlooking the canyon and sat down in a chair. It hit me then. *Oh my God, I killed a man today!* I didn't I have any choice, did I? I had always thought that this could be a possibility, but it was happening. The Old Man was right.

"You look kinda worn down"

It was the Old Man.

"I had to shoot someone today, I killed him." I said, "I don't think I am handling it very well."

I reached over on the table next to me and picked up my little pipe, lit it and took a hit off it. I offered it to Chris. He shook his head no. He sat down beside me.

"Jeff, I hope it is the last time it happens. But it very well may not be. Try to look at it this way. When I came back from Vietnam for a good fifteen years it ate me alive. The dreams were horrible. I could see the faces of every man or woman that I killed up close. For a time, I blamed myself. Guilt ate me alive. Finally, a really wise man I knew told me to get over it. He made me understand that I was a tool, and had I not pulled that trigger, it would have been me that died. You didn't make that man come down here and attack your friends and shoot that woman. He did it on his own, and he would have shot you for a candy bar. It is survival. You owe it to your neighbors to protect them and serve them, just as if you were a policeman."

"Yeah, Chris. But they were just hungry."

"Jeff, it doesn't matter. They chose to use force. We will feed what we can, if they come peaceably. But we can never allow force to overcome us. And, by the way, you need to be on top of all the people coming in. This could turn bad too, if not led properly."

As he finished speaking Nell came around and sat down in my lap, leaned in and put her head on my chest.

Chris laughed. "There, that's what you need! Make him feel better Nell. He's feeling kinda down!" And he walked away.

Nell nestled in and said, "I heard what happened. I am so sorry it came to that. I know you had to do it. you are a good person, you would not have done it if it wasn't necessary. By the way, Billie is much better. She is going to their RV."

I answered, "That's fine. She will be more comfortable there. Her kids need her right now near them. Oh, something I wanted to tell you. I have been avoiding it, but here goes. That day at the waterfall, I accidentally walked up on you and Marion. I didn't want to embarrass either of you so I retreated. But, anyway, that was one of the most beautiful sights I believe I have ever seen."

She laughed her musical laugh.

"I know, I saw you. That was a very gentlemanly thing to do. Thank you. I would not have wanted her embarrassed either. It was her first time with another woman. She said she had wanted to do it for a long time. We had talked about it a few times. But that day, with us riding double on Smokey and our bodies kinda moving together, it just happened. I just love her so much, she is so sweet. So, you approve or disapprove?"

"Oh sweetie, just as long as you are still in love with me and want to be with me, I would never disapprove of anything that awesome and sweet. Does James know or suspect, or would he disapprove? For a while anyway, we have to be careful of anything that would disrupt the status quo of the community. Feelings are going to be on edge. It's gonna be antsy for a while. We have a lot of work and planning to do."

I was awakened before daylight the next morning with a hard shaking. It seemed to go on for minutes. I ran outside. Everyone else had the same thought, all in various stages of dress.

We all gathered, discussing what may have happened. Some thought one of the Denver refineries exploded, but I figured we would see the glow of a fire from them. Others said a bomb, maybe another nuclear bomb. But we would had seen that, too, I thought.

It was coming daylight. Someone said, "Hey, let's have breakfast. I will cook."

I turned to look at Dave, standing with a spatula in each hand. A hurrah went up. Everyone went back to their dwelling to bring food to be prepared. That's good, I thought. Something to create unity.

We had scarey finished breakfast and volunteers were cleaning up when the shaking started again. I timed it this time. Eighty-seven seconds. Then fifteen minutes, and another sixty seconds of shaking. I had no explanations except an earthquake. But where? The shakes seemed to ripple from the east, but it didn't make any sense.

All the talk that morning was about the big shakes. A few more happened from time to time, throughout most of the day, but none so severe as the first ones. Another day went by with no news reports. I was starting to feel all alone.

Mid-afternoon we were planning food

rationing and sentry duties, all the little details about securing our compound. I heard something. I listened. It seemed to be coming from the south, I picked up my rifle, and walked around the deck. There it was, the familiar wap, wap, wap of a military helicopter. It came from the south. A Black hawk. It passed to the east of us, then banked to the left, circling tight to the north then circling west and coming in low. We waved. Someone in the door waved back. It hovered above the canyon just off the deck, closer and closer. Then this cameo clad individual and two carbon stamps like him simply stepped out of the door onto the deck.

"Good afternoon Folks. I am Major John Fitzgerald, United States Army."

The Black Hawk moved away and circled off just a short distance away.

"Good Afternoon, Major. I am Jeff Bartlett. This is my wife, Nell. These are friends and neighbors. How may I help you?"

"Well, Jeff, methinks we both need a lot of help, but I don't much know where it will be coming from for a while."

The major went on to relate that they were trying to ascertain where pockets of the population were, and what their conditions were. He was from Fort Carson. He also said they were about to abandon the Fort because of the riots and hoards of people storming them looking for food, fuel, whatever, to aleve their desperate condition. He asked how we were. We told him we were fortifying our position, and preparing to survive as long as possible.

The major went on to say that if any kind of control could have held the people together many more would have been saved. He said basically that anarchy destroyed and was destroying them.

I asked him about the shakes this morning. He said, "You don't have any communication?"

I told him our TV feed had only been sporadic.

He hesitated, then spoke slowly. "Jeff, folks, this is hard for me. Most of my family lived there. But the shakes this morning you felt were, well, the New Madrid fault broke apart. There isn't a city left standing from Iowa all the way down the Mississippi. The storm got everything south of Vicksburg. The earthquake has leveled everything else. Funny thing though," his voice quivered a bit, "the arch is still standing at St. Louis. Everything else fell down, but it's still standing. I don't know if that means anything. The water got most of the people, anyway. No one was prepared for something like that. No one seems to know why it happened now. The seismologists have been predicting it for years. Maybe all that water, I don't know. Coincidence, maybe. I must be going. I just wanted to check on you folks." He smiled. "You're the first one that haven't shot at us. Good luck, stay vigilant. There are some bad people out there. God bless you, and God bless what's left of the United States."

He and his men walked to the edge of the deck. The Black Hawk backed in to the edge of the deck the men hopped on. The Major turned to us and came to attention and offered a sharp hand salute, and stepped aboard his dark green bird. It turned away and was gone up the canyon.

After that little interlude we all sat down on the deck. Several of the women were crying. What was happening? Was it the end of the world? Oh, wait, yes. The world had ended as we knew it. But we were still here. And we had food and shelter. Now, next how to protect it.

"Chris, I know you were in combat. How many other vets present?"

Two other hands came up.

"Chris, some of my thoughts. Number one. If we have people approach us, and they don't respect our privacy, they try to force their way in, my thoughts are, they must be killed. I can't believe I am actually saying this. But if we let them go, I think they will come back in force. I know how bad it sounds and how bloodthirsty. But it seems logical."

"Jeff, you are right. However, we have to temper this. We need to give everyone a chance, but still exercise caution. The Major said that people were shooting at them in their chopper. This just shows the level of desperation of the remaining populace. We will eventually be discovered."

We were planning the best way to confront a crowd of hostile people when one of the walkie-talkies screeched.

"Motorcycle rider coming in, he has stopped at the barrels and is waving, doesn't appear to be armed."

I answered back, "Wave him in!"

A few minutes later a biker topped the hill and

turned up the road to the compound. We watched him cautiously as he came to a stop, killed the bike, dismounted and took off his helmet. A handsome young man in his late thirties appeared.

"Jeff, don't you recognize me?"

I looked carefully.

"Oh My God! David, I didn't till now!" I ran to him embracing him.

"Man, I didn't know if you were dead or alive, it is so good to see you!"

"Everyone, this is David Suttle. I have known him for twenty years. He is a veteran of both Iraq and Afghanistan. David, this is Nell. And I told you about Chris. And James and Marion, Mike and Shelly, and, hell, there is no way you can remember everyone. Oh, yeah, another Dave, here."

As Dave Love came forward with a glass of ice tea. "Here, David, thought you might be thirsty."

David nodded and took the glass of tea. "I was. Thanks, Dave."

We all settled around the deck and began to ask questions of the man that had come from the outside world. Food was prepared and consumed. A newly full moon looked down on the little settlement in the Rocky Mountains, dazed, somewhat confused, but determined to survive.

David described his journey from Fort Hood, Texas. He had just completed his last enlistment when the bombs fell. He decided now was not the time to reenlist, and decided he would come to see me. As the chaos ensued afterward the journey became difficult and perilous. He kept off main roads and avoided cities and towns. Near the end, difficulty obtaining fuel became his major problems. Sometimes he would find abandoned cars and siphon from them. He even helped a couple of farmers protect their livestock and took his pay in gas. He said his bike was on reserve when he headed up to Fortress Rock. We filled a bowl of some good sensimilla, and toasted each others good fortune.

"Jeff, I like your sentry idea."

"Thank Chris. It is his idea and creation. Chris is a Vietnam Vet."

David acknowledged Chris by raising his glass of tea.

"Thanks, Chris. I read a lot about Vietnam while in Afghanistan. You guys had some shitty duty and a shitty thank you, and a shitty homecoming. I salute you. You know what? The same game plan was used in Afghanistan at the start as was used in Vietnam. CIA covert operations, then Special Forces, then a slow troop build up, then support personnel. And with about the same results." He thought for a moment. "I guess we won't be doing that for while anymore, will we?"

"David, we had a visitor this afternoon. A Major from Fort Carson. He told us a lot of what has happened, told us about the New Madrid Fault breaking, causing the shakes."

"Oh Shit! That's what that was! Damn, like, insult upon injury. Is there anything left?"

"Yeah, the Arch at St. Louis. That's all, he said."

"Damn. All those poor people. Now I guess Americans will know how those Afghani and Iraqi people felt when their country was destroyed." He paused. "Funny thing is, they are not taking it nearly as well. After all my time there, I never felt as insecure around civilians as I have the last week or so. We really are a brutal people."

He looked up, as he seemed to come back to reality.

"Any trouble here yet?"

We told him about the incident down off the mountain. He said we should prepare ourselves, that the guy we had let go was going to mean trouble for us eventually. Chris and I looked at each other.

"David, would you like to work with Mike and James, and yes, Chris, to tighten up our security?"

"I would be happy to. But first someplace to spread my bedroll. I haven't slept much in the last few days."

I pointed in the living room.

"There is a daybed over under the window. It will do for tonight."

Somehow, the young man's appearance had helped my attitude. Some professional help made me feel safer. I joined a sleeping Nell, who snuggled her sweet body closer and sighed.

I was awakened early by the sound of a couple of ATV's. I raised the bed room window curtain to catch a glimpse of David and Chris heading out down through the meadow to the south. Nell was already up and out. I made me some oatmeal and honey, and went out on the deck to watch the morning unfold with the shadows on the faces of the cliff on the other side of the canyon.

I had loved this place from the very start. It had been something of a refuge from the outside world, now it was a refuge from a now suddenly hostile world.

Nell and Marion emerged from the greenhouse, their blouses stuck to them from sweating. I wanted to ask if it was from passion or planting, but refrained after seeing the dirt on their hands.

Nell came and set across the table from me. Marion joined her after washing their hands.

"Jeff," Nell asked, "is there anyway we could enlarge the greenhouse? We are going to need to grow more food, with the extra people we are accumulating. Some things we can grow outside, maybe some down in the canyon. But we are going to need more food. I think our stores will get us through the winter, with some stretching, but we need to start looking to the future."

Marion nodded in agreement. "Shelly and I have gardens and small greenhouses, if we can be assured of protecting them. We are a little ways from the main compound here."

"Yes, I think so. I will discuss it with the other guys. We need other building materials as well. We will probably wait until winter and make a raid on Fort Collins, maybe the population will settle itself by then. It is much too dangerous down there now. You two and Shelly, and whomever else you can recruit, plan out a food rationing plan. If you need any help, just ask."

Nell answered, "Thanks, Babe. And, by the way, I told Marion that you were aware of our love affair and it is all OK, that she didn't have to hide it from you."

Marion beamed. "Just don't you love her to pieces. I always knew there was something missing in my life, and Nell has helped me find it. You are the greatest for accepting it and approving of it. I don't know yet if I can tell James." She frowned slightly. "I love him and don't want to hurt him or our relationship. Time will tell, I guess. OK, back to work girlfriend!"

October 17, 2043

As we now are nearing the mid century mark, and I am past my three quarter century mark, I think a lot of those early days of the destruction and chaos. We thought all that would happen, or possibly could happen, had happened. Little did we know that it was only the beginnings of our planet's tribulation. Our planning surely did save us, but somehow it was just dumb luck that we made decisions that just some how worked out. And some of the predictions the scientists had made in the early parts of the century didn't quite happen the way they thought they would.

The Yellowstone Caldera, for example, didn't do exactly as predicted, or we would have all been goners. I look now on all these little children, none of which carry my blood, but I lay claim to them all. I have watched them be born and grow in this time of evolvement of man. I believe in their future. I believe the systems of laws and regulations we have set forward to guide us will have the ability to evolve as we evolve as a people. Our schools are based on teaching the children how to learn, not forcing a rhetoric down their throats that will inhibit thinking. Some of our technology is coming back. Not all of it was lost. Shelly McCollum, whom I had known as a young wife and mother from before the first days of chaos, had been instrumental in the new school organizations. In it's earliest days, we had few people as teachers. With a big need for the surviving children to be educated, and to deal with their young minds, with the trauma they had endured, she had devised plans to where the more apt students were given their task as tutors of students that perhaps didn't learn as well. Her ideas worked not only because no student was left behind, but also because the tutoring students developed leadership skills, and an ability to think outside the box. It helped them to see things that impaired other student learning habits and be able to correct them in themselves. Older people were encouraged to write the history of their time and the time we lived in. And to remember as much from their parents and grandparents. A few books were left, but not many. Many were used to burn and create warmth for first winter of Chaos. So many died that first winter. But something worked. Our educational levels soared, higher than maybe twenty to forty years before Chaos happened.

So much was changed, even after order returned. So much was destroyed, that we didn't have the manpower or the resource to be rebuilt. A great new respect for mother nature had developed. Oh well, give an old man a break. We all ramble a bit, time does that. Now back to our story. How it all happened, what we endured, what we learned, the people we came to be.

David had arrived at a good time. We updated him on our discussion on when to use deadly force and when not to use. He had ideas about that.

In Afghanistan, he said, it was always a guess. Whether someone approaching you was a young boy, full of curiosity, or a terrorist, with the face of a cherub. He said this will be no different. He says that after a while your gut will tell you, that you will develop a sixth sense. Oh, yes, mistakes will be made. You may harm some, and some may try to harm you. He said that is where you learn to use teams. You always have back up.

Our next discussion was allowing new people in to our community. We were less than forty total. We needed more numbers. But who and how? And we can only allow what we can feed. Too, we needed people with skills of all kinds. I said we didn't want more than a hundred to one hundred fifty the first year. Everyone seemed to accept that. A few days later we had the opportunity to test our theories. One of the high up sentries called.

"I see people on a farm tractor pulling a wagon. Also a team of horses pulling a wagon, with some riders. They are headed this way. Be a while, they are moving slow."

I thought for a moment. "Hold all fire. Let them come close. We are coming down."

I yelled for David, James, and Mike. "Arm yourselves and lets go!"

I started the Dodge, all jumped in and down the hill we went. Across the creek around a couple of curves. I told David, "You guys back me up."

I got out of the truck. I still carried my forty-four revolver in it's holster.

I walked slowly down the road about fifty to sixty yards, and stopped. I waited. Soon came the slow rumble of a diesel farm tractor around in view. The big John Deere appeared almost as an anachronism, in my opinion. The team and wagon, then about six riders. They came forward to about fifty yards and all stopped. The engine on the big tractor idled quietly. A tall, slender man, early sixties, jumped down from the tractor. He wore denim jeans and shirt and a western hat. A younger version of himself appeared beside him. They walked forward to within about ten feet of me and stopped.

The older man said, "Afternoon. I'm Charlie Wells, my son Randy," gesturing towards the younger man.

"Afternoon, Jeff Bartlett. Mr. Wells, sir, I must advise you are entering a closed community."

"Oh, Sorry to hear that. We are looking for a place to settle. It isn't safe out home anymore. Any suggestions?"

"What did you folks do before this mess all started?"

"We had a ranch out near the Kansas border. Did different stuff. Wife was a schoolteacher, daughter a nurse. There are twenty-one of us. We all were busy people."

I looked at the ones I could see. I motioned back and waved towards my companions.

"I want you meet some of my neighbors."

Both the men looked uneasy. I turned, "Don't worry, we mean you no harm."

About that time, the guys drive up. I turned and started smiling. They all picked up on it right away. As they walked up I introduced everyone. I told the guys about the Wells family. We all shook hands. By that time, several more of the family had approached us.

I turned and asked, "Charles, are you prepared with stores for the winter?"

"I think so, we have always tried to stay ahead on things."

I looked at my neighbors and friends carefully.

"Charles, if we were to invite you to join our community, you think we could work together and get along?"

The man smiled."I betcha. Cause you're about the first that hasn't shot at us. You seem like good people. I would be willing to give it a shot. Now let me ask you. Are you well prepared?"

"Yes, sir. We are in pretty good shape. We are forty strong. Your twenty will bring us to sixty. That will give us a bit more cushion against attacks. But it is absolutely essential that we have a community without friction for us to survive."

Charles looked me straight in the eye, "It sounds like a plan."

I turned and said, "Mike, drive everyone back up to the compound tell them we have people coming in. Have some refreshments prepared. I am going to ride in with them if it is alright with Mr. Wells."

" No, not unless you call me Chuck!"

"Chuck it is."

I followed him up onto the big John Deere and we headed slowly back to Fortress Rock. I explained to him about the road getting steep in the last half mile. When we reached the hill, he had the team unhitched and left the wagon. Some people rode the wagon horses, some doubled on the saddle horses, some of the kids climbed into the big tractor and up the hill we went. He said the back wagon could be brought up later, as it was mostly a passenger wagon. We arrived at the compound, refreshments were served, and everyone introduced and told their stories. Two of the boys were sent back with the tractor and brought the other trailer up. Horses were staked out in the tall grasses of the south meadow.

As I sat on a bench with Nell, watching the fire burn, I turned to her and said, "Sweetheart, our family is getting bigger, and you didn't even have to go through labor!"

She punched me and said, "Yeah, but that's no reason to not practice getting pregnant."

I squeezed her and said, "I'm ready!"

The question came up a few days later about community land, what belonged to whom, and what rights still belonged to the individual. So we decided to have a community meeting. It seems I had been elected as spokes-person to answer all questions. This was difficult. I didn't have all the answers.

Within a few weeks, as would have been considered normal, petty differences had begun to arise. So and so says this belonged to him, or he should be able to do this.

We decided at our first meeting to elect a

council that would meet weekly to decide grievances. Mike McCullom, James Roberts, Charles Wells, and Dan Nichols were elected to council seats. David Suttle was chosen to be Constable. Chris was asked if he would be an adviser if needed, to which he consented. We also appointed foraging committees and construction committees. Nell and Marion had recruited several women to help with harvesting and canning for adding to stores. Mike and James began planning for fall hunting trips for game.

Charles and his group had brought some badly need tools with them, including a small portable forge, an anvil, and other tools. We immediately began setting up a blacksmith shop. One of his sons was an excellent farrier.

Landowners and neighbors gave permissions for our crew to go and disassemble small out buildings and move them up to the compound. Soon our community began to take on the aspects of a small town.

The meadows below us to the south were rich in native grasses, and provided food for our horses and other livestock. Some of the younger men and a girl or two took shifts of tending them and not letting them wander. We took down fences from abandoned ranches nearby, and moved them up and fenced some pastures. All was looking well. Then, it happened.

I was standing on my deck, the early September air had a scent of fall in it. I heard a shot ring out from the rock tower to my east. Then, another. And another, lower down. I stepped to the big bell on the deck and started it ringing. Within minutes about 10 armed men were headed to observation points over the canyon. The gunfire continued, then there came the sound of an AK47 assault rifle. My walkie-talkie crackled.

"Jeff, about twenty or thirty people in the canyon! They are attempting to spread and climb up. They have rifles, and an assault rifle. Your orders?"

"Shoot them! They have decided to use force," I yelled. "David, did you get all that?"

"Roger that, Jeff! They're not coming up!"

For about a half hour sporadic gunfire echoed up and down the canyon. Someone said, "They are pulling back!"

I answered, "Watch them, make sure they are not leaving anyone that can sneak in after dark."

David said, "Jeff, we are doubling the guard for the next time, I won't say how long."

"Good Idea."

No one on our side had been injured. The guards said they thought a couple of the insurgents had been wounded, but didn't think anyone had been killed.

Charles said, "They will be back. They will

think because we are organized we have things to take, so they will be back."

" 'Fraid so, Chuck."

Early next morning, Mike, came racing in on his ATV.

"Jeff, there are a bunch of people coming up the south side of the canyon to the east. Can't tell how many."

I yelled at one of the girls to go ring the bell. Seconds later the bell is tolling. Horses were quickly saddled and soon a force of eighteen neighbors were armed and headed to meet our invaders. We stayed in the timber until we got to the meadow of James and Marion's place. We stopped and waited. In just a minute or two, about twenty men and women appeared over a slight rise. I waited until they came abreast one of the barrels with the sign Chris had put up. I lowered my rifle and took aim at the big circle's center. I squeezed the trigger. The .30-06 bucked, and the people immediately hit the ground. I watched through my scope. In less than a minute, one of the men pulled off his white t-shirt, stuck it on his rifle barrel, and started waving it.

I yelled, "One person, come forward, unarmed."

The guy stood took the shirt off the rifle put it back on, laid the rifle down, and started walking toward us, his hands in the air. I stood up behind the boulder I was using for cover, David was continuing to watch the others through his scope.

As he approached our position, I noticed him to be a young man in his mid thirties. Reasonably in good shape, a bit dirty and sweaty, but who wasn't. He seemed slightly familiar, but I didn't quite recognize him.

When he got within about fifteen or so feet, I said, "Stop there. You can lower you hands."

"Thanks, Mr. Bartlett. You don't recognize me do you?"

"Well, you do look familiar. But I can't quite put my finger on you."

"My name is Arne, short for Arnold. I used to check you out sometimes at Home Depot. I even hauled a load of material up here a few years ago."

"Of course! You have to understand, life has been a bit extraordinary lately. What can we do for ya, Arne?"

"Well, Mr. Bartlett, I quit Home Depot about a year ago and moved up to Laramie to go to college. The Army was going to pay for it. Then this happened. These people with me, they are friends of mine from Laramie. We have banded together for survival. I told them about this place, and you, and that old man that was helping you. I figured that if there was anyplace that would make it, you would."

I thought for a moment. "Arne, were you with those people that stormed us yesterday?"

"No Sir. But we did hear it. They are still there, but they moved down the canyon a bit beyond where we were. A couple of us sneaked down on them last night to spy on them. They are planning on coming up on you from the south, they are waiting for more of there friends to arrive. They are a bad bunch, Mr. Bartlett!"

"Loose the Mr. Bartlett, it's Jeff. Arne, call your friends up. If you don't mind, we are going to keep your weapons for a while till we get to know you better. It isn't my rule, it's a community rule. When did you guys eat last?"

"Yesterday morning, kinda. It wasn't much. We caught a couple of rabbits. Weapons are ok, we don't have any ammo left anyway, to speak of. Coupla' rounds or so."

He turned and waved for his friends, who stood and started forward.

"Thanks......Jeff. I owe you. We will help any way we can contribute, we were about ready to give up."

Shortly, about eleven more guys and about eight women joined us. Most of them in their mid twenties, or later. We collected their weapons and started back for the Fortress. Upon arrival, we took them to the deck where they were fed. We offered them a place to shower and refresh themselves. They all had tents and bedrolls, and by afternoon had found a suitable camping area in the forest. Just before sundown they once again appeared on my deck.

Arne said, "Jeff, we don't intend to be a burden. Could you line us up some chores? We want to carry our own weight."

I returned, "Arne, I appreciate that. The girls can always join in on food preparation and kitchen duty. Or, for that matter, anyone can, especially if you are talented in that field. Dinner will be served here in about an hour. We have decided to have communal meals. Food seems to stretch farther that way with less waste. You can always help with clean-up. But first, would like introductions and a bit of history on each of you."

By the time that was finished, dinner was set out and I was quite satisfied we had increased our numbers to about eighty with good, talented, stable people. Most of them were educated to a degree and most of them talented in many fields.

The next morning the sounds of galloping horses shook me from a sound sleep. I pulled on a pair of jeans and ran outside just as two of the herd attendants came riding up and did flying dismounts. The first to land in front of me was Susan, one of Chuck's band.

"Mr. Jeff! There is a large group of people sneaking in from the south through the meadow, staying under the trees. They didn't see us, we led our horses away until we were below the crest of a hill then beat it back here. They are a mile or two away."

"Thanks, Susan. You guys go get some breakfast."

I quickly rounded up about twenty-five or thirty of the men and we set out down to the place I had named 'The Fairy Glen', a narrowing box canyon just south of us. We took cover along the rocky top. About fifteen minutes later a large group of men and women appeared, all of them armed, moving into the little canyon and headed for the single trail that topped over toward our camp.

I watched them through my scope. The guy out front was carrying an AK-47. Probably the same one I had heard two days ago. They were all dressed in militia like cameo gear, bearded unkempt, tough looking people. I turned to David.

"Can you take out that AK? Make things a bit more equal. You don't have to kill him just disable his gun, make him know we mean business. Wait until he stops the next time. He looks out of shape and tired after his long walk."

"Gotcha," was David's reply.

I went back to my watching. As they neared fifty yards, well into the canyon, I motioned my guys to surround them on both sides, putting them into a crossfire.

A minute later the leader stopped, setting the butt of the AK on his knee. Seconds after that, David's rifle cracked, and the AK went spinning.

They all squatted and ducked.

I rolled over between the two boulders and said in a loud voice.

"You people evidently have a death wish. This the second time you have come at us. There won't be a third. I want you to lay down all your weapons and ammo, and do a one-eighty out of here. If we see you again, we will shoot first. We are prepared."

I rolled over and raised up. As I did, I saw a

weapon come up pointing at me. I dropped and as I did, a bullet bounced off the boulder near me. Then more fire from below. They didn't stand a chance, our men cut them down. When it was over only a young boy about fifteen and three women were alive and unharmed. They were unarmed. I was glad to see our guys spared them.

We walked down to the battle field. Most everyone was sick at what had happened. We gave them a chance. They chose not to take it. We questioned the women and boy, all were from the Loveland-Longmont area. They told a harrowing story of bloodshed, rape, and the horrors that come with a catastrophic event such as we all were experiencing. The women said they were going back to find relatives. We warned them against coming back. They said they would not.

The boy walked to me and said, "Please, Sir, can I stay here? My mom and dad were killed by these guys. I had a sister. But I don't know where she is, she was away at college. I don't have anywhere else to go, and I don't want to go back there!" pointing back to the south.

I looked at David. He nodded yes. Most everyone else nodded as well.

"Yes. But understand this. You have come at us with a hostile force, you are going to be under close watch. What's your name?"

"Eric, Sir. Eric Mattern."

"Ok, Eric. I once knew some Matterns down in Texas. You can team up with David here. Do as he says, and we will get along good."

The next chore was to be a gruesome one. We had thirty one bodies to bury. We found a spot about fifty or sixty yards out of the canyon that was soft enough to dig in. Remember, this is the Rocky Mountains. We carried all the bodies up and laid them out. We left a couple of guys to watch them and make sure no animals came along to feed on them.

We arrived back at the compound and related the story. Several people volunteered to go back on the burial detail. Shovels and picks were loaded onto a wagon and hooked to Chuck's big tractor. The crew assembled and left on their grisly detail.

About then, two or three girls from Arne's group came up out of the canyon from the spring. As they approached, one of them let out a piercing scream and came running, shouting at the top of her voice.

"Eric! Eric! Oh my God, Eric, you are alive! You are alive!"

She grabbed the boy hugging and kissing him, and he was hugging and kissing her as well. Both of them crying. As soon as they had calmed, Eric turned to me.

"This my sister Meg, Sir. I really owe you now. You have saved her too!"

"Well, don't give me all the credit Eric. Others helped her, too. Like Arne, here. I am glad you two have found each other."

I turned to see lots of people wiping their eyes. We all had lost lots of family, friends and people in our lives. Many that will only live in our memories. It was a good moment to see these two united.

At dinner I sat by Arne. As we ate, I felt to ask him.

"Arne, do you think anything is left at Home Depot?"

"Absolutely, Jeff. Those mobs aren't trying to build anything. And the others are just hiding out, trying to survive, just stay alive. That isn't easy either. You can't really trust anyone. You remember back in 2012 and '13 and '14, when those dictators in the middle east all fell? It was the same thing. A few people banded together, but most of all they were cutting each others throats for a crust of bread."

"How soon do you think it will be before we could make a raid down there and get some loads of material and get out alive?"

He thought for a minute. "Probably mid-December. It has to get cold enough to keep them inside. Yeah, and they need to exhaust more of their ammo."

"Yeah, me too. We are going to do it. We need roofing supplies, glass, insulation, screws , nails, lumber. We want to build more greenhouses. It is a must for our survival. Also, I would like to build a distillation plant. Any thoughts?"

He looked at me, then turned his head toward one of the other tables. In a louder voice he called.

"Mannie!"

One of the guys that had arrived with him

looked up. Arne motioned for him to join us. The young man picked up his plate and walked over.

"What's up, Arnie?"

"Mr. Jeff here wants to know if we can build a distillery."

Mannie looked at me and said, "Well, I built the one at U of W in Laramie. What do you want to distill?"

"Hemp seed for one thing."

"Right on. That's easy."

He turned to Arne. "You know, with transportation, we could just go get that one. Probably no one in authority there to care."

That night, as we went to bed, Nell said that I should check in on the Old Man the next day, that he wasn't feeling well. I said that I would.

Chris was getting old, probably the stress of the last month or so.

Nell and I took a few minutes the next morning to talk. I related to her the events of the last evening with Arne and Mannie. Also some of the plans I had been thinking about for the last few days.

Her remark to me simply, "Jeff, I have known ever since I met you that you were a great man. I always thought from the very first time I met you, that I needed to tie my kite to you. You will be remembered someday in the future as another George Washington, or Abraham Lincoln. I knew from the first that if I didn't go with you, I would miss out on something special. I love you so much."

My throat got tight, tears came to my eyes. I was speechless.

"That Saturday, at TRF, was the day my luck arrived. I could never have done all this without you. You have motivated me, Nell, and made me happy. I am the one that owes the debt, and I love you for so many things."

We lay and cuddled until a knock at the door. I said, "Enter!"

It was Dave, with a huge tray of food.

"I figured if you two were staying in bed all day, you would need something to keep your strength up," he laughed.

"Wow, thanks, Dave. I haven't seen you much lately, sorry about being a bad host."

"Awe, you been pretty busy. And I haven't thanked you near enough for the invite. Hate to think where I would be right now otherwise. So thanks, man."

Nell piped in, "He has been pretty busy himself, him and one of Mr. Wells' nieces have fell in love, and he's cheatin' on me!" She stuck out her lower lip in a pouty look.

"Yeah, well, you and your cute girlfriend, you wouldn't miss me anyway."

"Kids," I drawled.

"Anyway, I'll leave you lovebirds alone. By the way, Jeff, Chris isn't looking so good this morning. Probably should check in on him. Bye now!"

After breakfast I walked out to the Old Man's trailer. I knocked, and got a "Enter". I walked into the small but neatly kept quarters. Chris was still in bed.

"Good morning, Pop. How you feeling?"

The Old Man's voice was weak. I wasn't used to hearing him like this.

"Morning, Jeff. I'm kinda tuckered out. Sit

down a minute or so."

"I'll do it, Chris. I've been kinda neglectful the past few days. Nell told me last night I should come see you. Then Dave again this morning. Been a little busy lately."

"I just bet you have. Don't worry about me, you have a lotta' people depending on you.

"Jeff, before I came up here, I had been feeling bad so I went to the VA hospital in Albuquerque. They told me that I have some problems with my heart. I don't understand the technicalities of it all, but they said without a bunch of surgeries I was living on borrowed time. I was still thinking about it when all this started. I made the decision to come here. I have had a good life, and I didn't want to go through all that medical stuff. I know people that have. It is a long healing process that sometimes doesn't even happen. It was my decision."

"Damn, Chris, I didn't know. What can I do to

help? Without you none of this would have been possible. You are the oldest friend I have, you have taught me so much. Did they say how much time you have?"

"No, but I know it probably isn't too much, just by the way I feel. I do have some medicine I am taking. But, I am just so grateful that I am getting to spend that time with you and Nell. And actually, with all these people. It is an awesome thing to see this community coming together with a common cause. And, Jeff, with such a great leader. I am so proud of you and the man you have become. I remember that scrappy kid that I pulled off of that motorbike in Austin years ago. He was so full of piss and vinegar, but had no direction. You have found that direction, and now you are sharing it with others. If I have had anything to do with that, then my life has had purpose, and I can say to myself, 'Well done, old man'. Jeff, I was almost eighteen when I wound up in the jungles of South Vietnam. I watched my friends die around me, or get blown up until they weren't even recognizable. I have sat with my poncho over me while agent orange came down on me like a spring rain. I watched as beautiful nature with trees and flowers withered away and became a land of utter desolation. The people who lived there wore constant looks of despair. They walked as if they were carrying the world upon their backs. Their manner of support was gone, their homes and farms and businesses torn apart. Then, one day, we got on a big airplane and we just flew away, leaving them worse than they had before we came, and so many never came back. And those who did, and are still alive to day - or were a few weeks ago - live with dreams that are almost three quarters of a century old. They were never able to forget. It was real until their dying day. Jeff, I have always believed in karma, and I have always believed that someday we would have to pay for all this. Maybe it's just our turn to pay up. I just hope that we come out of it better than those people in Vietnam did, and the people in Iraq and Afghanistan. And Egypt, and Libya, Syria, and where ever they lost their homes and lives. This is probably just the prattling of an old man, but it is just the way I see it.

"You and Nell and these people around me are the people that I am happy to have around me in my last days.

"Jeff, I am not afraid of death. Death is like saddling up a good horse and riding off into the sunset to a new great adventure. I have met death three times. He is only a scary doorway, not a destination."

"Aw, Chris, I love ya, ol' man! You have been my father, more so than my real one. God, who knows how I would have wound up if you hadn't jerked me off that bike. This breaks my heart to hear you tell me this. But you have taught me that life is a cycle. We all have our time on the big stage, then we have to make our final bow. Then another actor will take our role and do something different with it. Your role has been that of a teacher to me, a mentor, the person that has suggested that there is more to life than one perceives at first. You slowed me down in time to stop and smell the roses before I ran past the bush without seeing it, or worse, ran totally over it. I can only do you honor by trying to pass along the things you have taught me.

"But, you are still here, for now. And we are going to make your time an awesome time. So your only job from here on out is to make sure that we don't wear you out."

I walked back to my house. Tears kept coming out of my eyes. I finally was able to compose myself by the time I entered. Dave and Nell and Marion and James were sitting around the table. I took a chair Everyone was looking at me.

"Well, this is for mostly your ears only. He doesn't have a lot more time. He wouldn't want everyone to know that, he would never accept pity. But, I want us all to make sure, even if we must carry him at some point, that he is here for every meal. And every social gathering. Unless he just refuses. I want his last time to be a time of enjoyment. We need to organize some social things - music, dances, plays. Especially with the kids. It will be good for us, and he will love it. He loves our new family. I think it is something that he hasn't had much of in his life.

"We are bound to have some more bad times. We need to develop community activities, to get our minds off the bad. It is necessary to give us hope for our future."

Marion piped up, "Shelly would be great for this. She has lots of ideas about things of this type. Oh, by the way, she wants to start a school. She has been meaning to talk to you, but all this stuff that has just happened kinda pushed it aside."

"Tell her to come see me in the evening. I think it is a great idea. Also, find me one of the older girls. Preferably one that can type or do shorthand proficiently. Have her come catch up with me. No, on second thought, find me two. I need secretarial skills."

I found Arne at his camp after searching for a few minutes.

"Arne, ya got a minute?"

"Always. What's up?"

"It just occurred to me, there are probably other pockets of people somewhere. I would like to find some way to set up a ham radio station and start broadcasting. Any ideas?"

"I am on it. I will get back with you as soon as I find out something!"

"Get with David, he is probably knowledgeable as well."

He answered with a salute. I smiled. I met David as I was returning to my house and told him of my ideas. He agreed it was a good idea, and would find Arne.

I walked in just in time to catch Nell and Marion in a hug.

"Hey, you two, get a room. No, on second thought, come here. Nell, we have ice, we have some milk, we have sugar. Can we make ice cream? I would like to have an ice cream social tonight on the deck."

Marion answered, "Yes we can! We have an ice cream freezer, Mike and Shelly have one as well. What a great idea! After dinner, would that be good?"

"Perfect!"

I went into the greenhouse and picked my self a nice bud from the curing room and went back out to the end of the deck. I set my glass of tea on the table, filled my pipe, lit it, took a slow puff and sat down. I turned my small stereo on to a bit of Pink Floyd *Meddle* and picked up my note pad and started making lists of projects that would be necessary to keep a community of this size going and items we needed to make it possible.

I had decided we had to make some trips out before winter for some much needed items. I also decided that I was going to pass this on to others more fitted. David would lead them. Arne was ex-military. I needed a committee for this type of thing. Cool heads, good planners. I spent the afternoon writing and sketching ideas.

Before long my buzz had worn off and I had six pages of notes to digest with the council. About the time I was about to get up and leave I heard someone call.

"Jeff!" It was Shelly.

"Hi, Shelly. I was hoping you would come by. Got some things I would like to talk about."

"Me too, Jeff, me too!"

We spent the next hour going over ideas for artistic pursuits, cultural and social activities. I was going to brief her on the ice cream thing but she was way ahead of me. We talked about schooling. We had similar ideas about the way teaching should be done, and similar dislikes about the way it had been done in the past. I told her to put together a curriculum and to not limit ages so much. We should make school a place where anyone with the desire to learn should have the opportunity. She thought that was a good idea. I told her we were going to send out foraging teams, and for her to make a list of things that were essential to her projects. As we finished, she stood and gave me a big hug and said for me not to worry, everything would workout all right. I told her I knew that was true, and that I would have been much better in school had I gotten hugs from my pretty school teacher, for which I got a swat on the shoulder. It was just then the dinner bell rang.

As we walked back to the dining area, I saw the Old Man being escorted by two of the college girls. He had a smile from ear to ear. For a few days, I thought, the worst to be over. For a few days!

In the months after the storms and riots and the Chaos, we learned to deal with the present, and start looking toward the future. And, like all generations, we tended to forget the past and some of the things we learned in it. I had read and studied my self about how fragile our eco-system was. I had read about the dark times in our planet's history. I had even wondered, at times, how many civilizations had risen and fallen. I had seen items that had been presented as evidence that people had existed before and during the dinosaur period, items taken from lumps of coal that came from several hundred feet below the surface of the earth. One tends to forget these things in the course of daily life. We also didn't always heed the knowledge that scientists put forward.

It was later in the first winter that we realized something was wrong. It simply wasn't getting cold enough. A blessing in many ways, as we didn't have enough shelters. We had grown to over a hundred by now.

By the next spring it was evident something *was* happening. We started getting some television from time to time again. They talked about the waters in the oceans rising, and Europe experiencing a longer winter. I was puzzled. What was happening?

But, I must get back to the story. After all, the people are what is important, and this about them.

In October and November we had a couple of small groups approach us. One hostile, we managed to run them off. They had guns, but evidently were short on ammo. One came from north of Red Feather Lakes, they had been virtually living on wild game. They said that they had no problem with people trying to harm them.

They had been down almost to Laramie, said they couldn't find anyone. No population. Said they had met one guy that said some of the ranchers north of Laramie had banded together and were rebuilding their communities.

This gave us some hope. We had put together a ham radio, and had someone monitoring it twenty-four seven. We would broadcast twice per day. As of yet, no one had answered. We were concerned about the weather, it was unseasonal for this time of the year. We finally sent Mike and a party of the hunters out to bring in meat. They were gone about three days and came in with three elk. This was not good, we needed cold weather for them to be able to hunt, and to keep the meat frozen till they could get back to our storage.

Thanksgiving came. We had a dinner. It was 85 degrees.

December 12, 2022

I arose about seven a.m. I walked out on the deck, and looked toward the overlook. There in the chair was Chris, wrapped in a blanket, sitting looking out over the canyon. I walked over to him.

"Chris, would you like to have some coffee or tea?"

He looked up, "No, Jeff, I'm fine. Jeff, they are

all there."

I looked out at the other canyon wall. "They who, Chris?"

"All my buddies, from Nam. They are waiting for me." He looked at me, "I love you Jeff, I have to go. Goodbye for now, I will see you soon."

He closed his eyes. I could almost feel his spirit rise up and head out across the canyon. I sat with him for a while, waiting, not wanting him to be gone. But somehow, I knew he was happy now. Once again he was young. He could run and jump and do all those things he had been able to do so long ago. I squeezed his hand. I realized that a part of my life was gone.

He had took his bows and left the stage. Now the understudy was left to take the role, and do his best to magnify it in his own way. I pulled the blanket up and covered that magnificent old head, where all the ideas for the Fortress had sprung from. Where the force that had shaped my life and character had come from. *No tears for you Chris, you go do something great now, face that next challenge. We will meet again!*

I walked back inside. Dave was in the kitchen, Nell was just coming out of the bedroom. They both looked at me, obviously seeing something in my face. I looked back, "Chris is gone."

"Gone where?" they both answered in chorus.

"Gone to be with his buddies from Nam," I said.

I smiled, "He is finally not the Ol' Man anymore. He is the young man once again. He pasted away, and his spirit flew out over the canyon. I felt it go."

They both came and we put our arms around each other and hugged. "I know we can't stop all the tears, but he is happy now. We can miss him, but let the tears be of joy for his release from pain and strife."

Dave and I went out and carried Chris' body inside and covered it.

Dave said, "I will go get the coffin later, after we prepare him."

"What coffin?"

"Oh, he had me make him one over a week ago."

"Yeah, he would have." I smiled and touched the old head lying in front of me.

Later, when breakfast was served and eaten, I asked everyone to stay for a moment. I walked out and stood in the midst of the tables.

"This morning, shortly after seven a.m., our dear friend, my mentor, Chris, shoved off for his next adventure. We will have a service for him tomorrow morning. He left us with a big responsibility, to maintain our community, which he dearly loved." Tears were beginning to fall, and sobs were heard. I turned away and walked back inside, before I started to cry as well.

The next morning I went to Chris's trailer. Still neat, clean and organized. I wanted these new friends to know something of the man I once knew. I felt totally uncomfortable as I sorted through his papers, belongings, collections of his eighty-odd years. My search lasted for hours, and I felt my loss more and more. I thought I knew the old man. But I knew so little. Where he came from, what he had done. I had missed so much!

I found pictures of a little boy, with a smiling mom. And a stern looking, proud looking father. They looked like people of late 1920's or early 30's, would guess just after WWII. I would guess the little boy to be three-ish. The dad looked like a veteran, it is sometimes easy to spot a vet. Then a death certificate - his mom. He was about seven. Early 50's by then. Dad, for some reason, enlists back into Army, he goes to Korea, twenty-three months. He is killed. Chris is living with his grandparents. They seem to be people of quality. Here is a Bronze Star, for his dad, and a Purple Heart. Chris graduates high school 1962 - diploma, National Honer Society. WOW!

Three years at CSU in Fort Collins. He was from here, I thought so.

Enlists in Army in 1965. Three tours in Vietnam. Retires rank of Master Sargent. Oh My God! Two Silver Stars, three Purple Hearts. Other medals that didn't know what they were for.

Then, here a notebooks of writings, essays on all kinds of subjects. Philosophy, science, environmental issues. Sociology. He must have written volumes.

Then the books of poetry. Pictures of a pretty girl wearing late 60's early 70's hair style, taken in Austin.

Pictures of The Fortress in its early days. Pictures of me and Nell. I sat back in the chair.

My hands were shaking. I had to go and tell his story in a couple of hours. I felt as weak as if I had been ill.

I stood in front of my neighbors and friends and I looked at them.

I said, "It is my duty to stand here today and tell you a story. It is a story about a man who changed my whole life, starting about thirty years ago. It is a story about a man that is responsible for this place where we are living now. Without him, it would not have been here. If I had told you this story yesterday, it would have been much different. You see, I have known this man for all these years, yet, I only knew one small part of him. This morning I learned about the rest of Chris, the parts he never talked about. I was going to come up here and try to make my self reserved and shed no tears. To hell with that, I am going to tell you about the Old Man, and we are going laugh and cry and celebrate his life and create memories that won't ever be forgotten. So here goes.

"Christopher Bowen was always in my head as 'the Old Man'. He was born Oct 29, 1945, probably some where near here or Fort Collins. His parents were probably working class, his mother passed away when he was seven. He was raised by his grandparents, his dad was killed in Korea in 1953. He was decorated for valor. Chris graduated high school in 1962 and he went to CSU for a couple of years. Then enlisted in the Army in 1965. He did three tours in Vietnam. Ladies and gentlemen, his medals." Several *'Ooo's'* and *'Awes'* were heard. I continued, "Two Silver Stars, three Purple Hearts, others I don't know."

I set the stack of notebooks on the table. "These are his writings. On many different subjects. These will be made a part of our library, so that we may all study them.

"Then there is the poetry. I tried to read this when I first found it, I couldn't then. I can't now. I would not be able to talk.

"Poems about the men he served with. Poems

about being in the depths of despair and finding a leg up start a new life. Poems about death and pain and life, and about new births, and laughter, and joy. Poems describing wildness' and jungles and mountains that he saw the beauty in, even some of them in the midst of war. Poems to a girl he fell in love with, that for some reason I don't know seemed to slip away.

"I was being a complete asshole, riding my motorcycle through a bunch of people, watching them move, the first time I saw him. He jerked my young ass off the bike and sat me down and had a talk with me in a very respectful but critical way. He changed my life. He had me come to Colorado and buy this place and advised me in so many ways. He was and is my hero. He will never die in my memories, he will always be a part of the fortress. We will not view him today. Instead, we will all remember him as he touched us. Rest in Peace, my friend. Go party with your buddies."

Chris is buried just on the west edge of the main house of the fortress, on a rise, that looks out over the canyon that he and I loved to gaze upon. The golden eagles will fly guard patrols past his resting place. In the fall he will be serenaded by the bugling of the bull elks during the mating season. He will watch the first snowflakes fall every winter, and listen to running water babbling as it melts in the spring, and I will able to look out at his grave every day of my life, here in this changed new world.

That afternoon, my loss still weighed heavy. I went out to my favorite place on the deck overlooking the canyon, in the chair that Chris had sat in as he jumped the bonds of mortality and raced into that great adventure that none of us can be spectators to, in hopes of feeling something of his spirit still there to comfort me. As I sat trying to make sense of it all, I noticed down to the right of me a flash of white. Then it disappeared. Then, there is was again, moving toward me in the late afternoon shadows. I watched and slowly the form of a medium sized white dog appeared. He came closer and closer. As he came around the rocks below the deck, he hopped up onto one and turned and looked at me very straight for a long time, his black ears up and turned forward, his black nose twitching, as if he was trying to recognize some one or something. He paused, then jumped the six or so feet to the floor of the deck. I had remained seated. He walked to my left side, looked up at me, and lay down beside my feet and lay his head on his paws and sighed and relaxed. He was rather skinny, but seemed healthy otherwise. I recognized his breed as being, for the most part, Australian Cattle Dog, or Blue Heeler, with maybe a little something else. I figured he was hungry.

I turned and looked down and said, "Hey, Amigo." He jerked his head up and looked at me, cocking his head to one side. "You hungry and thirsty? Let's go get some food." I got up and turned to head to the kitchen, the dog was right in step as we went through the door. As I entered the room, Nell said, "Well, who do you have here?"

"He said his name was Amigo."

Nell knelt. "Hello, Amigo."

Amigo lowered his head and ears and seemed to smile a hello.

"Nell, we need to find our guest some food and water. Any ideas?"

"Jeff, I have plenty of good leftovers. He should like some of them. Come with me Amigo!" The dog followed her obediently.

She first set a pan of water down for him. He

drank conservatively, then looked back at her. The next bowl was full of meat scraps, some pieces of bread, and a couple of elk ribs with some good meat left on them. We took the bowl out to the deck and sat down at a table and gave Amigo the bowl. He sniffed it all over, took a couple of licks, then looked up at Nell, as if to say 'thanks', then proceeded to eat.

We watched him as he ate his dinner, he wasn't a woofy eater. He examined each part of the food and ate it slowly and carefully, chewing before swallowing. When he came to the ribs he picked each out carefully and laid them aside, then returned to finish the bowl and polished it carefully with his tongue.

He next turned his attention to the bones, cleaning them swiftly. He then in turn took each bone out to the edge of the deck and left them together. He returned and drank a bit of water, then came and lay down between our feet, he sighed a big sigh, then rolled to his side closed his eyes and went to sleep. Nell looked at me.

"I believe he's home!"

I answered, "I think so!"

We sat for an hour or so, watching the Rocky Mountain sky fill with stars. The sounds of the camp provided a peaceful background. Somewhere on the edge of the forest, someone was playing a guitar and singing a cowboy song.

I took another puff on my pipe and passed it to Nell. She took it and set it aside.

"Jeff," she spoke very softly and quietly, as if afraid someone would overhear, "You don't think Chris had anything to do with Amigo showing up when he did?"

"Nell, we won't even go there."

"OK. But he is so amazing. He is so quiet and respectful, he acts as if he know us!"

I looked at her.

"Ok, ok, but I can't help thinking it!"

I wouldn't dare voice it, but I had been sitting there wishing Chris back when Amigo appeared.

Dave L. and one of Chuck's nieces came around the corner and up on the deck. Amigo sat up quickly. Dave asked "Well, who is this?"

"Dave, meet Amigo. He has decided to join the community."

"Hello Amigo." Dave and the girl both knelt. Amigo wagged his tail and stepped forward to greet them. They offered their hands. He sniffed them, then returned to his position between Nell and myself.

"Jeff, you know Sam here, don't ya?"

"Indeed I do. How are you, Samantha?"

"Fine, Mr. Jeff!"

I laughed. I still was a bit uncomfortable with these expressions of respect from the younger members of our society.

"Jeff, I have been telling Sam about the drum jams we had at TRF and other places, and I was wondering about making some drums and maybe doing that here. What do ya think?"

"I think it is a great idea. If you remember, Nell and I got acquainted at one of those at Ed's house. We will bring it up. If the community don't want it all time right here, we have a whole mountaintop. Go for it."

"Great. I have two with me. I can use those to teach others how to make their own. You know, stimulate a little creativity."

Dave and Sam jumped up and ran to his yurt and quickly emerged carrying his two djembe's, and disappeared into the edge of the forest. In a few minutes the guitar playing stopped abruptly. Then, a minute or so later, a single drum started. Then, another minute or so, another started, and joined the rhythm of the first. Something inside me said *this is fitting*. Amigo sat up and listened, the black ears peering into the darkness intently. He then relaxed and lay his muzzle onto his paws with his ears still up listening. I though of one of the papers the Old Man had written in a spiral note pad.

"I thought of original man, sitting in the edge of the forest, watching the stars. It is too early to sleep. His belly is full, his pet wolf is asleep near the campfire. He lays back and slaps his full stomach. He likes the hollow sound, he slaps it twice more. He picks up two sticks of wood together and strikes one against another, it has a tick-tock sound. He thumps his stomach with one hand, and hits the stick with another. Then he realizes hours have passed. And drumming was born. Soon his neighbor, who was listening, joins him and socialization was born. A tradition springs forth that will last beyond the generation that have followed. "

"Right on, Ol' Man."

Nell, having preceded me, I rose to go to my room. As I did, Amigo stood and looked up at me and turned to follow as I entered the house. I went to my room and proceeded to undress and get into bed. When I did get horizontal, he followed me and lay down beside the bed. A sad, contemplative, uplifting, reflective, good day had ended.

April 30, 2023

Spring came in early, but it was more like summer. Little rain fell. We had had almost no snow. We forbade any fires except in the inner compound. It was limited to whatever was absolutely necessary, and only if there was no wind. We decided to put out some extra gardens down on the middle fork of Rabbit Creek. We built a little shelter down there for the game watchman. We found some ground and cleared and planted potatoes and turnips and garlic and onions. On a sandy spot we planted watermelons and cantaloupes. We were a little high in elevation for them, but we decided to try anyway. Up on top, we made more gardens along what was the South Fork of Rabbit Creek. It had some springs that rarely surfaced.

It was to be a hot summer that year. David took out three different scrounging parties. The first one was to Home Depot. Arne had been right. It really hadn't been damaged or vandalized. After the chaotic behavior of the previous summer that had decimated the population, most every one had calmed down as far as violence was concerned. Everyone that had survived seemed to count themselves as lucky.

Summer Solstice was set for our large community meeting. We all gathered that morning for our various committees to report. Security reported there had been no insurgent episodes in over sixty days. Discussion opened as to whether it might be safe for some of the families locally to return to their own homes. I thought it might make food production more productive, but I was concerned about splitting our stores. We decided all should be free to go.

But for the time being, food would be prepared and distributed at the compound, where you went to eat it would be your business. It would keep the community together, but give us a bit more space.

June 29, 2023

Dave L. came running out of the radio building yelling, "Some one's broadcasting!"

I headed for the radio. As I entered I heard Dave S. saying, "Glad to hear you folks are alive Max. Here, let me introduce you to Jeff Bartlett."

"Hi, I'm Jeff Bartlett. Who's this?"

The voice on the other end identified himself as Max Adkins. He was out side of Laramie, near the town of Centennial. He said they were about a hundred fifty strong now. They were doing about the same things we were. I asked them what they were in need of, he asked if he could get back to me, and for me to make a list as well.

We talked twice more in the next two days. They said they had cattle and goats and some horses. We had some extra foodstuffs we needed to put to use before they became to old. They also needed some medical people, as they had some sick people. By the end of second day we had set up a trade agreement. We loaded two wagons and headed out on the third day. Early in the morning we came out of Rabbit Creek and headed toward US 287. We traveled all day, seeing no one. About five in the evening we stopped at the old Virginia Dale Stage Stop. We backed our wagons up to the building about twenty feet apart, unhitched the teams, removed their harness' and tied the horses in between the wagons. Crossing the tongues of the wagons, we used some old timbers to complete the temp corral. We fed them a bale of hay we had brought along. and watered them with a couple of 5 gallon plastic buckets we had filled at a creek a ways back. It wasn't plush, but they would make do. We had just sat down to have our evenings rations when the voice of an old man rings out.

"Hey, strangers, you got a bite more to spare?

I ain't et most all day."

We turned to see a grizzled old man approaching us. He was wearing canvas Carhardt overalls and boots, and he was carrying a sizable backpack.

He walked up, and droped his pack.

"Evening. I'm Austin Day."

"Well, Mr. Day, I think we might find something for ya."

I reached out and handed him a canteen of water. He took it, drank some and wiped his mouth with his sleeve.

"Thanks, I needed that."

We gave him food and sat to watch the sun setting over the mountains to the west.

Austin was one of the people you became

used to seeing walking along the sides of highways all over America in the last fifty-sixty years. Always looking at the next horizon, never content to stay too long in one spot. His lifestyle had probably saved his life, because he was not content to live in the midst of humanity. One sometimes is led to consider if they might be occupied by the spirits of the original hunter-gatherers. Society called them 'homeless'.

It was not true, they were very much at home.

Austin told us stories. He said he was leaving Chicago when the storms hit. He had journeyed across Iowa, then the Dakota's. He said there were still people around here and there. He said what the mobs didn't kill and who didn't starve to death, were starting to look to their future.

He looked down at his feet, and laughed a little.

"I wonder how long any of them will survive. They have been raised up not knowin' anythin', not how to learn anythin', everthin' wuz done fer them. They went to Walmart to get their food and their clothes. They pushed a button to heat or cool their houses. They didn't know how to fix anythin'. Their cars were takin' care of by somebody else, if they were takin care of at all. All they knew how to do was put gas in'em. They need leadership if any are to survive, and there ain't much of that."

Truly a man who has become a student of human nature in his wandering. Knowing we had a long day ahead of us, and needed to rest, we excused ourselves. We did ask Austin his plans.

"Aw, I'm gunna go on down here a ways and get some sleep, an go see what Denver looks like now."

We wished him safe journey, gave him some water and some food. He picked up his bag and turned to walk away, then turned back.

"Y'all good folks. Ain't many left. Y'all take care, now, ya hear?"

Next morning, we climbed the grade up to the state line. As we topped the rise, there lay what looked like half the world ahead of us. Here we left the Highway and headed in a north-westerly direction toward old Centennial. All day we drove seeing nothing but pronghorn, a few deer, and a black bear. Then, as we were nearing the foothills leading up to Libby Flats, we heard a noise. We look up along the ridge. There was about twenty horses all running parallel to us. As we passed, two riders topped the ridge and head down toward us. We located our weapons. As we got closer, we could see it was a girl and a guy, probably in their twenties. They rode up saying, "You must be the people down near Fort Collins. I'm Mat, this is Molly. These are some of the Horses you might want. We rounded 'em up for you to see."

"Hi, I'm Jeff Bartlett. This is Dave Suttle," I introduced everyone.

"You guys follow us up here aways. 'Bout a mile, there is an old ranch. We have a small camp there."

We rode a while, then we topped a little hill and found an old ranch along a dried up stream. The horses were herded into a maybe ten acre pasture. The young couple were unsaddling their mounts.

As we arrived, Matt said, "You can put your horses in that corral over there. There is hay in the barn over there. We will stay here tonight. It's about half a day to our little town."

I walked to the fence where the horses were held. They were a mixed bunch. Several different breeds, a couple of drafts, several quarters, and several of who knows! I thought to myself, *what a strange thing, finding these animals a necessity, once again*. Old men in Austin had told me when they were young everyone rode horses, as there were few cars. I had lived through a period of automotive transportation, and seen it die, as horse drawn had died. Now, horse drawn was back. Question was, would autos ever come back? Yeah, I'm sure, somewhere there was yet alive, a scientist who was crying, "OH! The Earth has saved itself! No more carbon emissions! We are saved!"

I found it difficult at the moment to take comfort in that. Wasn't sure it would save us either.

Diana, our nurse, who was traveling with us, walked up.

"Mr. Jeff, you about ready for food? It's about there."

" Yes, of course. I was just lost in the past for a minute."

"I think we all do that from time to time. We are at a special point in history. I just hope it gets recorded so the people in the future will know to keep this from happening again!"

"That's very astute, Diana, and I hope that's right as well. Come on, let's go eat."

I put my arm around her, and walked into the old ranch house.

After a delicious dinner of crackers and elk chili with frijoles, washed down with cold water, we sat around an old pot-bellied stove that stopped the evening chill. Diane and David did the dishes. David never seemed to relax and have much enjoyment, he took his job of keeping us safe at top of his list. It was good to see him laughing and playing with the pretty young girl. I looked around the cabin. It was built of solid logs chinked with mud, and maybe something else more modern. I looked at the posts and beams. It was lofted and had room for several people to sleep. It must have been well over a hundred years old.

We were still experimenting with our distillery. We needed a fuel source. The gasoline, even where we could find it, didn't work real well, thanks to the refinery processes in the early twenty first century. It went bad pretty quick. The diesel lasted a bit longer. We had more now than before. With the help of hand pumps we emptied a lot of service station tanks. It didn't seem to work in the small engines as well as big ones. When we could get our chainsaws working we could build cabins like these. I settled back in an old chair and soon dreams of Nell danced through my thoughts as I drifted into a restful sleep.

I awoke to the smell of coffee brewing. I had never really liked the stuff, but was surprised. I didn't know there was anymore. The girl called Molly was at the stove.

"Molly," I said, she turned and smiled," where did the coffee come from?"

She replied, "Oh, we have some things, here and there. Would you like a cup?"

"No, thanks, dear. Never developed the taste for it. Just curious." I walked out and found a hiding place behind the barn to satisfy nature's urges.

When I returned, Diane and Molly were handing out burritos for breakfast. I had one with some frijoles and went and caught the horses. Today I would get to see another group of people that I had not seen before. I was beginning to think that might never happen again.

Mid afternoon, after a short pull up a long grade, we came into a small valley with a beautiful creek running through it. As we entered the valley, shouts rang out from several points.

"Wagons coming in! Matt and Molly are back!"

As we pulled up to a long log cabin, a man in his mid to late fifties came out, hand extended. "Hello, I'm Max Adkins. Good to meet you."

"Hi, Jeff Bartlett. Same here, Max. Great place

you have here!"

A crowd had gathered, curious to greet new faces, as curious as we were to meet them. We spent a short while with introductions and pleasantries. Max and I found us a comfortable bench in the shade to talk. The conversation went from the horses to needs of everyone. They had a few solar panels to use to power the radio, but their batteries were growing weak with usage. I suggested harnessing the creek with a water turbine. Max thought it a good idea, but said he didn't have anyone that was that tech savvy. We did. We decided to set up a manpower exchange between our towns, kinda like military TDY duty.

I told him about our scrounging trips for building supplies in Fort Collins, and removing plate glass windows from big stores and offices to build greenhouses.

They had not had any real news from the outside world since the storms, not that we had had that much. None, actually, lately. Something to do with the inability to adjust to satellite drift. We knew the west coast was still there, but as yet no communication with them. He was shocked when I related the New Madrid earthquake information. He shook his head, and wiped the tears from his eyes.

That evening we had a community meeting. Myself and David and Diane and Charles Wells Jr. and the three others that had traveled with us were introduced to the general populace. We answered questions as best we could.

When I related the story of the visit of the Army Major, and his story of the earthquakes, loud gasps and 'Oh No's' were heard. Several people left the group crying uncontrollably. I assumed they had families or loved ones that lived in that region. I also told them of what had happened to the east coast and south. When my talk ended, it was a somber crowd that looked back at me.

I thought perhaps after all that, it might be fitting to speak a few words of encouragement. I started by saying, "Folks, I am aware of the sadness of the stories I have just related. But we must look at this as a new beginning. Our country was in desperate straits. It seemed to be stalled, it's growth limited. I daresay, there are few men or women here that were happy with the status quo in the last ten years or so. I see many children here in your group, as we have several in our community, and I have no doubt in the coming months we will discover other little islands of humanity, and link with them. So let's pool our resources and our minds and our talents, and create a new better world for them. It is our duty, you know, so let's take it on with an excited positive attitude, with a renewed vigor. Before I die, it is my goal to see our communities establishing a new country. Since the world of oil and oil energy has been kicked in the teeth, and since we are having to create our world from the grassroots, let's find a way to do it with renewable, sustainable energy.

"Let's start a new educational system which will educate all these young people with practical knowledge, that is established from truth and not from whatever power that happens to be in charge dictates. Let's teach them how to learn, and arouse their natural curiosity and see what happens. Thanks for inviting us to your city, we have found things here to inspire us. We invite you to come visit us as soon as you can. Good afternoon."

As I turned away, people started to applaud. Then louder and louder. I turned back to face them, and saw everyone standing on their feet. I bowed slightly, and said, "Thank you so much, you honor me!"

Max stepped forward, shaking my hand.

"Thanks, Jeff, that was great talk. You have given me a renewed vigor for sure, and wow, my head is suddenly full of ideas! I like the idea of our towns working together. By the way, I have some forestry maps. Let's see if we can map out a shorter route between us."

The next day was full of preparations for the

trip home. We had decided that only one wagon would go home with us. Max and his crew had discovered a wheat and oat field that had been planted and deserted, but had sprouted back of its on accord. They were to harvest as soon as it would be ready, and would share with us. A welcome addition to our precarious balancing of our stores.

Max and I poured over the maps and found a new route probably cutting off fifteen or twenty miles. We were taking back twenty head of horses with us.

Morning the next day found us loaded and ready to leave. People came and shook our hands, promising visits as soon as possible. Promises to forge ahead in our new life. Diane was staying for a while to help with medical issues, and to try to help set new ideas about healthy diets where possible. One of the other young men, an engineering student by the name of Lynn, also stayed to work on some of their techie projects.

Amongst a roaring goodbye, we moved out

toward our Fortress Rock. We were accompanied by Matt and Molly and another young couple. I'm sorry, but time and memory have taken their names from me, but not the memory of their service to us. We tied a couple of the horses to the wagon, the rest were ponied with the riders or ridden by David and another of our party. Our new trail took us almost due south for most of that day. We kept to the meadows, and followed the terrain. The going was easy enough. Still, twice we found ourselves at a place where we had to backtrack for a mile or so in order to get the wagon through. We kept steady in our pace and about dark came out on a narrow gravel road. A sign down the road a bit said FS165.

"Bingo," I said, "the rest of the way is roadway. We did it!"

We stopped and tied the horses on a tether and broke a couple of bales of hay or so. They had been watered in a creek just minutes before we found the road. We snacked on rations prepared in advance. We set up shifts to watch the horses, and crashed and burned till just before dawn, until the horses started making noises and getting excited. We jumped from our bedrolls and ran to calm them down, whereupon we found a Ma bear and two cubs had gotten just a bit to close. We arose and and set off again. This time I had maps. We were able to trot the horses for short periods, making very good time. We watered as often as we thought necessary, noting trails and watering holes for future reference. About a mile down the road from where we stopped was an abandoned ranch house, with several good pens, and a barn. We marked it as an overnight rest station. Couldn't help but wonder what had happened to the owners. We moved more rapidly today than yesterday as we passed through the town of Red Feather Lakes. On the east side of town we came to an old convenience store. As we approached, two men stepped from the building with shotguns leveled. Almost as one we pulled up and our guns were leveled at them.

Hoping this wouldn't turn into a shootout, I

shouted, "Put down your guns, we mean you no harm!"

The older of the two answered, "How about taking some of your own advice, and do the same. We are only defending ourselves."

I motioned for everyone to lower their guns. As they did, the two men did also.

"My name is Jeff. We have a settlement down east of here, we are just passing through."

"Brian and Danny here. We are the last people left in town, and that is a fact."

I got down from the wagon and walked over and shook hands with the men. Their eyes belied the desperation they felt, and the chaos they had witnessed. They had the thousand yard stare of a combat vet. Their demeanor was that of men that their world had left them and had no future. They spoke of the days after the storms when hundreds of cars had came up the highway to escape the rioting and mayhem in the cities down below, but instead of escaping it, had brought it with them. They said that those that didn't kill each other last fall, fighting over food and shelter, died during the winter of starvation and illness' that was partner to it. I asked them what had been their lives before the world had shaken its coat like a wet dog drying itself. They answered that they had both been professors at CSU. They were gay men, but had never felt a part of the militant gay community. They had kept a small cabin outside Red Feathers until it was burned by rioters. They barely escaped into the forest. They were educated men, but they were men well acquainted with nature, and knew how to survive. People that would be valuable in our community.

I asked them, "How would you two feel about joining our community?"

Brian looked at me, with just the hint of a smile, and maybe the birth of a twinkle in his eye.

"Are you sure we wouldn't be the main course of a family dinner when we get there? It wouldn't be the first time it has happened, you know."

I was totally taken aback by his question.

"Oh my God, NO! You don't mean to say......" my voice trailed off. They both nodded yes.

"Oh Jeez-us," was all I could reply.

Danny spoke up.

"What are you looking for, from us?" Both men truly wary of others, obviously of good reason.

"Danny, Brian, we are trying to rebuild our society based on equality and everyone working together. We have just linked with another community up in Wyoming. These folks are with them," pointing to Matt and Molly and their friends. "We would like whatever you are able to contribute - your knowledge, your talents, your strengths, your abilities. We need everybody, but we need everybody at work."

The two looked at each other. Brian asked, "Where can we ride?"

"Find you a spot on the bags there. Secure your shot guns, don't want one of those bad boys going off and hurting someone."

Almost dark found us about three miles from the Fortress. I could see the white bluffs reflecting in the setting sun. It was after nine p.m. before we wound our way up to the compound. I saw a white flash and Amigo was sitting beside me on the wagon seat licking my face. He was followed by Nell, and she seemed to be emulating the dog somewhat. Amigo had gone to see the new horses and people. When I could get my breath, I exclaimed, "I take it you are glad to see me?"

"Oh God, I didn't think you were ever getting

back! And Amigo would have starved in another day! He has sat in that chair at the edge of the canyon and watched for three days."

Amigo was back rubbing on my legs. I patted his head and knelt and rubbed his head and scratched his neck. It was then I became aware of the others.

"Nell, this is Brian and Danny, Matt and Molly. I will tell you all their stories later. First, everyone is starved, and we need to find sleeping arrangements for everyone."

"Dave and some of the others are setting food out as we speak," said Nell, "come, everyone, I am so happy to meet you. We will get acquainted over dinner."

As we came around the corner of the house to the deck, a big round of applause went up. Dave hollered, "Welcome back everybody! Welcome to all you strangers! Dig in and we will talk later."

After we had eaten it was plain to see that most were tired. The young ones were pulled away by others their own age. Brian and Danny came and sat with us on our deck. When I returned from the curing room with a nice sativa bud, I thought they were gonna kiss me. That made me nervous. I am a pretty liberal guy, but I have to draw the line somewhere.

Danny spoke, "Jeff, we have lain and talked for weeks on how good it would be to have some of that wonderful plant. It would have gotten us through some rough times had we been able to find it. God Bless You!"

I filled the bowl and handed it to Brian. He put it to his lips, almost reverently, and lit it, inhaling as he did. He held his breathe, passing it back to me. I shook my head, pointing at Danny. He then passed it to him. Then the bowl came to me. I had been thinking of this for days. We sat in the starlit Colorado night and talked for an hour about life and philosophy and art until, I could see, that the day had won and we needed rest. I pointed them at the showers, and told them to sleep in Chris' old trailer. We woke Amigo up from his snoring nap and headed for our own shower and bed.

I awoke early morning and there, sitting astride me, was this beautiful blonde girl dressed as God had dressed her the day she was born. She had always been the beauty in my life and this morning was no different. As she sat above me and moved her body, I realized that pleasure with her each time was a new experience, always worth repetition. The look of rapture on her face led me to believe I must have something to do with it. And as we reached the peak of our ecstasy, I felt I would never be able to love anyone else the same way.

As we rolled over and lay breathless in each others arms, I was able to voice, "Thanks, I needed that!"

"OH yeah! I needed that, too!"

"What's the matter? Dave and Marion desert

you?"

She giggled, "Dave is in love. Love is in love. We talk, but it doesn't feel right to either of us. And Marion is a whole new thing. I love her, but it is different than you."

About that time the bedroom door kicked open and a white body appeared between us on the bed. Sitting up, black ears erect, and looking at us with almond colored eyes intently.

We both echoed, "Good Morning, Amigo!"

His tail wagged and he broke into a toothy doggie grin. We looked at each other. Must be time to get up.

Charles and his group had a couple of extra saddles, but we were short on all kinds of tack. We decided to do a re-con on ranches within a ten mile radius of us. The Wyoming couples and a couple of Chuck's people volunteered. They took a couple of extra horses as pack animals and set out. On the second day they were back, loaded with gear but not on pack horses. They had a covered wagon with them. They had found this older couple late on their first day. They had added twelve saddles of different types, a couple of pack saddles, bridles, halters, bits, blankets, reins, and lots of other horse paraphernalia. The older couple, the Elliott's, had been living on an isolated ranch and had been protected by their isolation. They were out riding when they met our kids. They looked like they had been taken right out of a western magazine, with their big hats and leather vests and chaps. Ben and Ellie were in their late sixties and early seventies. They had been married for over fifty years, and had raised six children. Ellie had been a school teacher at the Livermore school for years. I remembered Livermore School as a small school grades 1st through 6th. They had no idea what had happened to their children and grandchildren, but feared the worst.

We had notified Max and his clan of our safe arrival. The day the kids came back, we received an excited radio call from Max again. They had radio contact with another community near Walden, Colorado, a small community of 50-60 people. They were wanting to relocate, winters were too severe for their resources. I suggested they come back over Cameron Pass down a bit lower on the Poudre River, that way they would be close enough to interact. Max agreed. An hour later, he came back.

"They want to know if it's safe, as over half of their party are women and children. They say they have only a limited amount of ammunition, and are afraid of running into hostility."

I called for David. He came and I told him about the situation. He asked me how far it was. I told him about ninety miles. He said it would take over three days to get there, maybe four. I called Max back and told him the people were about ninety or ninety five miles from us, and part of that was cross country, but they were only about sixty five from him. He said he would get back with me.

David and I decided that even though the people at Walden were farther from us, that it would be better for them to come our way. So when Max called me back, we co-ordinated a rescue plan. He would take our wagon, and some horses, and one of his wagons with some people and go to them. We would leave and go the other way and meet them on Cameron Pass in five days. Then we would assist them in coming down and setting up another community. David selected 3 others to make the trip to Cameron Pass. Nell said she wanted to go this time.

Next morning we saddled up and left early. Six riders and three pack horses. Amigo was in and out along the trail, obviously enjoying the travel. We headed west-southwest, crossing Livermore road about an hour later then follow it until we were below the ridge, skirting Grey Rock. We followed the contours of the mountains all day guided by a topo map of Roosevelt National Forest. Sometimes following one of the many county roads, sometimes making our own to cut distance. We finally came on CR 69 and followed it south. Late afternoon found us on the banks of the Cashe de Poudre River just below what had been Glen Echo Resort in the community of Rustic. We moved upstream to the bridge and crossed. We moved among the buildings and the old store, finding no signs of life. This is where we would move the people from Walden to. It would offer shelter and be close enough for us to help support them. The elevation was just a little over 7,000 ft. It was perfect.

We unsaddled and unloaded and set up camp.

Nell and I walked down to the river and sat on a rock. The river was quite low for this time of the year. Even Rocky Mountain National Park got little snow, so there was little runoff, but it was still water, good water. I had an idea.

"Nell, we should move our community here. We have water. Look at the pastureland for livestock. We are too crowded at the Fortress."

"But Jeff, I rather enjoy everyone there. I have gotten rather used to the people."

"Yes, but it is for the good of the people. We are taxing our spring. We have no idea how long this heat and drought is going to last. We are short on pasture. Look, some of it is already fenced, there are some buildings here, it would be so much easier to rebuild. The danger seems to be over. I will bring it up to committee when we return home."

We took off our boots and jeans and waded in the cool water. Next thing I knew, I was walking with a naked lady. I laughed, "Wwell, it's pretty sure no cars are coming by to surprise you."

I took off my clothes and pretty soon we were laughing and squealing like two carefree teenagers. I looked up and there stood the other four. What could I say?

"Come on in, the water's fine!"

It took no encouraging. Boots and clothes went flying, and merriment ensued. After we had played and redressed, we returned to the camp, as some were preparing food. I discussed my idea with David. He agreed that is was a good idea.

"Jeff, we could sustain two hundred people here easily, look at all the cabins, along the river and up that county road. I don't know what happened to these people, but no one has been here in a while. If they come back, we will deal with it then. " I agreed with him totally.

Morning found us fed and headed up Poudre Highway. It was all up hill from here. We made good time, stopping occasionally to rest or water the horses. We stopped that evening just above the falls of the Poudre, which weren't near as impressive as the last time I saw them. We watched a meteor shower that evening that was outstanding, laying in our bedrolls, looking up at the night sky. I loved Colorado. There was always a show of some kind going on, Mother Nature saw to it. As I watched my thoughts turned to the changes in our heavenly body, the speed at which they were enacted, with what terrible results. Yet the heavens seem to remain constant, yet we know they are changing also.

What a marvelous and complex, sometimes terrifying universe, in which we live.

Next day, we left the Poudre as it turned and headed up toward it's birthplace, high in the top of Rocky Mountain National Park. By late afternoon we passed several campgrounds and arrived at the top of Cameron Pass, our destination. We took refuge from a afternoon storm in the deserted Ranger Station. We spent the evening telling stories from our past. It was a practice we had enacted months ago to bring strangers together and put everyone on an equal footing.

David was one of the last. He spoke slowly and with great feeling, first about his early life as a runaway, about meeting me and our conversations as I drove him home to a dying father. About working for a few years until his mother passed as well. He said at that time he had nothing. He joined the Army, it gave him a sense of belonging. Then came Fallujah in Iraq. He lost two of his best buddies there, but he stayed on out of a sense of unity with members of his unit. They all felt the responsibility to protect each others "six". As Iraq wound down he was sent to Afghanistan. By now he felt that the Army was home. It wasn't until the bombs were reported stolen that he decided he was getting out of it. Then all this happened and he decided he wanted to come see me. Said he was glad he did, that this felt like home. We all applauded him.

Finally, it was Nell's turn. She laughed and got to her feet. She told about her youth, about when she was seventeen she started working during season at The Texas Renaissance Festival, about all the fun and the friends, the costumes and the drum jams and the dances. And how the influences of the hippie folk had instilled in her a desire to live off the land, to live as green a life as possible. She turned to me and said, "Then I met this guy. He was young and handsome and different. I saw in his eyes a desire for me," she giggled, "not just my body either," she wiggled, "but for my companionship as well. When he told me about The Fortress I knew I had to go with him or miss out on something grand in my life. And I am so glad I did. I love you Jeff Bartlett, and thank you from the bottom of my heart for making this possible." She teared up and Amigo looked up at her and whined softly.

One of the new girls asked, "Nell, how long have you guys been together?"

Nell answered quickly, "Twenty one years, four months and eighteen days!"

"Awwwww..."

Next morning we found some pieces of plywood and some paint and we made a makeshift sign.

WELCOME WALDEN SURVIVORS

We sat it up next to the road facing the west.

And we waited, this was day five. We waited. It was best expressed about 3 p.m. by David.

"God, what I would give for a cell phone."

It was echoed by all. Still, we had to wait. 4 p.m., 5. Finally, about 6:30, we heard the whinny of a horse to the west. It was answered by one of our own. It was a lone rider. He came up, dismounted, walked up.

"You must be Jeff. They won't be here until afternoon tomorrow. they are a pretty beat up group, about half starved."

Another night on the mountain. It rained, then hailed. I feared for the people on the way up. We waited and watched. About 2 p.m. we hear a shout from the west. Then we see heads of people riding in a wagon, then the bodies and the horses, one wagon, then two, then three wagons. They were here. We all stepped to the side of the road to wait.

I could see Max in the front wagon, he raised his arms and waved. I waved back, as we all did. Closer and closer, I heard some of our group exclaiming "Oh My!" and "Those poor people."

As the wagons pulled up it became evident this was a rescue mission. The children were gaunt and thin, as well as everyone else. They had dark eyes and somber faces, looking not quite as bad as holocaust survivors, but certainly very demoralized people.

I spoke up, "Hello folks, I'm Jeff Bartlett. Let's get everyone out of these wagons and into the Ranger headquarters. We are going to have hot food for you and you can rest tonight. I know you have had a hard day. Tomorrow will be a lot better. Things are going to get better starting now. Come on now.

Nell and all our people started helping people out of the wagons. A couple of the women and an old man, were lying in the wagons quite ill. Dakota, our other nurse, was busy seeing to them. They were picked up bodily and carried inside. Soups and stews were being cooked on the big wood stove. Cots were brought out and set up. It took over two hours to get everyone fed and comfortable.

I stepped outside with Max. "My God, Max! I wasn't expecting this!"

"Neither was I, Jeff. The reason we are so late is we had to bury two before we left. An old woman and a little girl. They were dead in bed. I am not sure a couple of these will make it. Jeff, I have been calling on all my reserves, I am about at the end of my rope." He spoke with tears in his eyes.

"Yeah, Max, go get some rest. And tell your people to turn in, we will take over tonight. I have something to discuss but it can wait until tomorrow." He nodded, and went inside.

I stood for a moment, stunned and dismayed. We had been so lucky that I had been oblivious to the fact that people were living in these conditions. I looked out at the darkness. How many more were there? I remembered old Austin's words. *"They have never been taught nothing, and they don't know nothing, and they have no leadership, most won't make it."* I sighed and turned back inside.

Most of us were up all night. Some of them couldn't handle the food and it made them sick. We comforted and tended them until late. One of Chuck's nephews, probably the one I had heard in the night before, went over to a table and sat down. He picked his guitar, and started to sing. Nothing but a cowboy's herding song, meant to calm the cattle on a stormy night. But it began to work. People began to relax. Children listened, then began to nod. Mothers cuddled them and weary eyes began to close. As the melody of the lonesome cowboy's songs wafted over the crowds I thought, *When you think it is impossible to hope, hope rises up like a bird from it's nest, and starts it flight anew.*

I'm not sure where last night began and today started, but it did. Max and his crew woke renewed and began to help us with this morning food preparation. By shortly after dawn the wagons were hitched and horses saddled. Some of the riders had taken some of the children on horse back, where the horses were willing.

We headed down the road. It was down hill all the way. I rode beside Max's wagon. Nell had given her horse to one of the men, as well as Dakota had done, to attend the sick.

As we rode, I filled Max in on my plans. Especially now, these people need leadership and protection until they could sustain themselves. All day we went. I was reluctant to stop, with no place to really camp. Finally, we came to the old store at Kinnikinnick. We got everyone inside and comfortable.

One of the young men that had come out with us was a good horsemen and seemed to be very reliable. I called him aside.

"Glen, at daylight do you think you can find your way back to the Fortress, and get Chuck and some others to bring more supplies?"

"Of Course, what do you need?"

I said, "Stuff to make soups, condensed milks, you've seen what they are like. Tell Chuck if he is up to it, I could use his help. And Mike McCullum as well. You ride carefully, don't do anything dangerous. We will be at Rustic tomorrow evening or before."

As Glen went inside, Nell appeared crying. I said, "Whats wrong, Babe?"

"Old Margie died. She barely ate last night. I wasn't surprised, but I never had anyone die in my arms before. Jeff, she told me all her family were in a town called Cape Girardeau, Missouri.

"Jeff, she begged me to get word to them. All I could do was tell her they would know for sure," she sobbed.

I put my arms around her and hugged her. "You did good, sweetheart. That was the right thing to do."

Morning came. As we fed everyone I walked around through them and talked as I walked.

"Most of you folks know where the town of Rustic is here below us." Most nodded affirmative. "That is our destination. The town is deserted. It is close enough to our community for us to be able to assist you to get on your feet, indeed we are considering moving some of our community there as well. It is a good location. We can grow gardens there, there is shelter there, and most importantly, water. We will not leave you, be assured of that. We all have a lot of work to do, and we all have to pull together to make it out of this situation. Our community has prospered through unity. That is the key. We are establishing schools, and building committees and other creative efforts. We welcome you and your talents. Oh, yeah, it's not all work. We have social activities as well. The young cowboy last night was an example. It's all going to be OK again."

I was answered by a chorus of *thank you*'s and *yes, we will help*'s!

The ride that day was not so long. We arrived in the afternoon, stopping at the store and lodge at Rustic. It had a RV campground there. A few abandoned RV's were still Everyone unloaded the wagons, taking their meager possessions and most going and sitting on the bank of the Poudre, as if it would wash all their troubles away. I had remembered that most of the cabins still had clothes hanging in the closets.

It was a warm day, I yelled, "Hey, everyone! Women and girls go that way, men and boys this way! Get those dirty clothes off, and get in the river! You are about to be reborn!" I turned to the young couple from Wyoming, "Go find some soap in the store, I know I saw some. I don't care what kind, and bring it to the river. Hop, hop. Let's go!"

It didn't take a lot of urging. We raided cabins for clothes and soon we had clean people. They all came and sat around us. They seemed renewed. One of the men from Walden came forward.

"Jeff and Max, we don't expect to pay you. I don't think you would take it anyway, but we are with you whatever you need, we are with you."

That evening, we had our evening meal and after wards we sat and introduced ourselves all around. We told the new group who we were and what our goals were.

We asked each one for a name, and what their skills were, how much schooling they had and what they like to do. We told them it didn't matter how menial the task, if it was something they enjoyed, they would get first choice at that.

We asked them how much they knew about the chaos that had enveloped us. Most knew of the storms, but knew nothing of the quakes. When we told them, it was the typical reaction - tears and upset. We told them there was very few left alive down in the cities, that we had not been past Fort Collin, but we expected the worst for that area as well. The evening was social, and everyone mingled and got to know each other.

Max and David and Nell and I stepped outside. We discussed moving a lot of our community over here for convenience sake. Everyone agreed, Rustic had more potential than The Fortress for a large group to live and grow. I soon found myself quite weary, having not slept the night before. I found Nell and we slipped away to our bedrolls, and were soon fast asleep.

I awoke with a cold dog nose poking me in the shoulder. I rolled over, "Good Morning, Amigo. You hungry?" I raised up and there, at my feet, was a half eaten rabbit. "No, I guess not." I turned to wake Nell and tell her that Amigo had brought her a present. She wasn't there.

I dressed quickly and pulled on my boots. I walked around to the front of the store to find tables laid out and people busy eating, Nell included.

She looked up and smiled.

"Did Amigo find you?"

"Yes, did you see what he brought me?"

"Yes, indeed. He is a good boy, he is helping to find food."

I looked down. "Yeah, Amigo, good boy. Next time a buffalo or a moose, dude." He looked at me and cocked his head.

We took some of the stronger of the new group and went through some of the cabins. It was strange. In most cases the clothes were hanging in the closets, books and papers were on the shelves, but there was absolutely nothing left that could be used as food. They ran out of food and they left. But where did everyone go? Are they all dead? Hard to believe....

Way back in the nineties I had some friends who drove trucks hauling meat out of Greeley, Colorado. They told me once that one of the managers of one of the food warehouses for New York and New Jersey told them that if all the truckers and trains just quit delivering to them, they would have totally empty shelves in less than two weeks. I knew for a fact that probably on any day there was at least five hundred truck loads of foodstuffs brought in. If they eat all that in two weeks, then what would they eat, the second two weeks. I didn't think I wanted to know that answer.

We asked them to group themselves in families, then families that are friends. We selected housing accordingly. We tried not to waste any space.

About 4:30 p.m. we heard horses coming in. Soon eight riders and and three pack horse were crossing the bridge. I heard Mike, "Hey, Jeff! We're coming in, don't shoot us." I waved my hand. Everybody waved. Mike and Chuck and James and Marion and three others.

After a brief chat, I caught Chuck by himself. "Chuck, what do you think of this place?"

"Oh, this a great spot. Water, sunny meadows,

buildings, good level spots."

"Chuck, I don't want to lose you, but what do you think about moving your crew and maybe some others over here?"

"Jeff, that is a good idea. More room, more potential. If we all work together, we can lick this situation. That Max guy is alright, too. I like him. And, Jeff, those poor people. I wonder how many more are left somewhere. I have never in my life seen people starving before. Yes, I will do it. Oh, by the way, The Elliott's should be in here in their wagon about dark, they wanted to come."

"Good. I will have a bed for them in one of the cabins. They will be tired. I'll tell Nell to keep some stew warm for them."

David appeared about then with one of the Walden men. "Jeff, Leif here says we should go to Fort Collins and hit all the storage room complexes. He said we might find a lot of stuff that would be very usable to us."

"Excellent idea. Wish I had thought of it. Do it."

"Also, Jeff, I know you been real busy and distracted and all, but I am surprised that you didn't notice that!" He pointed.

I turned my head, following his point. Finally, I saw what he was pointing at. A fuel sign with the word 'Diesel' $4.46.9 per gallon.

"Shit, David. We gotta find the stick and stick that tank."

"Already did, it's almost full. We will have to filter it," he grinned.

"I love you man! Best fuckin' thing I ever did picking up that weird looking kid with the blue hair." I gave him a big hug.

February 4, 2031

It is cold. It is so very cold. The elk have moved into the lower valleys where they grazed two hundred years ago, before cattle. We even have a few buffalo with them. James Roberts, five years ago, met some Lakota Sioux and talked them out of four calves. No hunting is allowed for another five years. I am sixty three years old, or I will be in August. Aww, I must go back inside, can't stand this. The canyon is white, the snow must six or seven feet deep in the bottom. I have stayed inside most of the winter. Beginning to get cabin fever a bit. I turned and went back inside the warm house. Nell, was busy grafting some little plants together.

"What are you doing, love?"

"I am going to grow an apple tree in the greenhouse, hydroponically."

"Ok," I guess I sounded a bit skeptical.

"No, we did it over at the big greenhouse over

at Rustic. It works."

"Thanks to all of you for the knowledge to do that, we have a thriving community because of it. 2026 would have killed everyone, except for those greenhouses."

I sat down by the fire place and put a coal to my favorite pipe.

We had warning barely about the coming cold period. The storms in '22 had seriously damaged our ecosystem. The warm waters running back into the gulf and western Atlantic so warmed the Gulf Stream that it stopped. Now, all of Europe and North America were in a mini Ice Age, or at least we hoped it was mini. The last two seemed to be a bit warmer. But we were alive, and flourishing. Out of the three colonies we have now thirty five new children. We had found other colonies all over the region. The knowledge that we had attained enabled us to build ham radios and power them with solar and hydro power. We could now talk to others as they came online, or, I might say, line-less. We were able to share knowledge and ideas. We even found a colony in West Virginia. This gave us hope for the future, but also it made us more cautious and motivated us to try to influence the surviving populace that change was necessary. Learn from history, don't allow the same mistakes to happen again at a later time. We must learn to embrace technology for the good things it brought to us, and balance it with natural resources, so that we grow in a balanced way.

We had used the combustion engine to help us to build in '22 and '23, but we didn't allow its use for ordinary transportation. First of all, we recognized we didn't have that much fuel left, and we used it for only the most necessary work. We started building our dwellings out of mud clay and straw mixture – adobe. We built into hills with southern exposures, utilizing solar gain. This was especially so with our huge greenhouses. We needed time for our forest to regrow and we, for the most part, stopped all forestry, we watched the forest for dying trees and utilized them. We found an abandoned sawmill up above Red Feathers and relocated it closer to us.

One of our greatest discoveries was a building process, from ancient times, by mixing a pulp made from hemp with limestone and water, and forming it into bricks. It would draw carbon from the atmosphere and form in a substance as hard as concrete. Brian and Danny had discovered the process in some old history they were studying.

The past eight years had been difficult with the weather conditions, but had not stopped us. Our eyes were ever toward the future.

Idaho

Russ waited patiently, his rifle resting on the log in front of him. He kept his face away from the scope, didn't want to fog it at the wrong moment. Two young bull elk were making their way down the ridge in front of him. _God, it was cold!_ He waited patiently, he wanted to get them both. The families needed this meat. This winter wasn't as bad as it had been though. It seemed almost normal. _Ha,_ he laughed to himself, _normal for the North Pole._ The bulls were moving cautiously, maybe they could smell him, maybe not. They were moving directly to the spot he wanted them, a creek with an old logging road running along side. He could get at least three shots off if he played it right. He was glad it was just elk this time. It wasn't that long ago that they had been forced to shoot people. The horror welled up in him just thinking of it. They weren't normal people though, they were crazy people. People that couldn't cope with change after the disasters. His neighbors and friends told stories about finding human bones in cooking fires. He thought to shake his head.

No, come on Russ, focus. Don't move. The bulls' sharp eye could pick up any movement. *Come on, little calves, just a few yards more*. He waited as they reached his target point. He raised the cross hairs to rest just to the rear of the shoulder, a little bit lower. Easy now. He squeezed the trigger, the rifle kicked. He shifted his aim and chambered another round. The second bull froze for a couple of seconds then reared slightly and turned facing Russ. He fired again, the shot hitting square in the heart. Both bulls went down. Russ chambered another round, and sat quietly and watched them.

Damien heard the two rifle cracks, then silence.

He turned to Cissy and her husband Brad.

"Come on, guys. Sounds like there's meat on the table."

He swung his leg over Chino and headed up the draw toward the place where he knew Russ would be. He was proud of Russ. He was one of those gifted hunters, and a crack shot. The other two followed with the three pack horses. If others had learned their life lesson as well as Russ, there wouldn't have been as much hell to pay as there was when the disasters struck. But that all seemed to be behind them now. Life was still hard, but the real struggle seemed to be over. He wondered if the world would ever be the way it once was before this mess.

As they topped the rise and headed down to the old logging road, Damien spied his son coming down the hillside, hopping and sliding in the snow. As they met he was still thirty yards above them. Hhe stopped and yelled, "About a hundred yards down, at the bottom by the creek, two bulls!"

Damien gave his son a high-five sign and yelled, "That's great! You get a raise!"

Cissy yelled, "Way to go Russ! That's my bro!"

It was after noon before they got the two animals gutted and quartered and packed on the three horses. It was a good five miles back to their cabins, and it wasn't all downhill.

Dark found them on the last half mile. It was cold, so when they pulled up they just unpacked the meat and Cissy and Brad led the horses to the barn. They had already unsaddled and wiped the riding horses down and fed and watered them. They finished the pack horses, and was standing watching the moon rise when her dad and brother came out of the meat locker. Russ yelled to the necking couple.

"You two should get a room!" Damien smiled.

Russ was just getting even for all the harassment he had received when he and Misty had been newly-weds. Brad's parents had been killed in that first bad week. He and Cissy had been classmates in school, so he had come to stay with Damien and Sandy. It was almost given that the two kids would fall in love with each other. Tomorrow, they would share the meat with some of their neighbors. But tonight was celebration of today's hunt.

Russ had built them a ham radio set shortly after the disaster. They monitored it constantly. They received transmissions from all over the country except the eastern United States. It seems it was left mostly devastated after the terrible storms. They heard of many colonies in the Rocky Mountain region, and some in Arizona, and in California. But now California was having problems with rising waters. Also, part of Oregon and the Coast of California.

Damien thought many times in wonder that a series of storms like those that had struck the east coast could have such a devastating effect on all of the country. All they basically did was destroy the grid. The people were so dependent on that grid that without electricity and fuel and natural gas that they simply went mad and destroyed themselves. But tonight, something scarier was happening. Mount Rainier seemed to be awakening. He had been told stories about Mount St. Helens erupting when he was only about two years old. He didn't remember the event, but the stories were scary and in later years he saw the videos. They were east of Rainier, and would at the least get the ash cloud, if nothing else. What else could happen?

Tonight, Damien and Sandy were hosting dinner for their family and twenty-five of their neighbors. All the hunting party ridded themselves of their hunting clothes and the smell of horses and blood and donned clean clothing. As they entered, he was greeted by a loud, "Grampa!"

Russ's six year old came running and jumped into his arms. Little Todd was Damien's pride and joy. Misty rescued Damien from the wigging boy and he shook hands with all his friends and related the story of today's hunt.

After dinner and some glasses of wine. All were seated around the large fireplace. And the subject of the evening was broached.

"Friends, Russ and I have given this a lot of thought, and we are considering a big move. All the way down to Colorado. It seems the communities down there are moving forward at much faster pace than the rest of the country. It seems to be a safer area as far as natural disasters go. It is much better for growing food than here. We are already starting to see health effects from improper diet in the children here. Russ and I have not figured a way to do this yet. It is a long way and will be difficult. We could use all your help, I want you think it over. If you are interested, let us know. It isn't going to be an instant move. We have to plan for it.

૪つ

Our buddy Dave Love had gone to the Rustic community to live. He and Sam had made vows toward each other. They now had a baby on the way, and Dave seemed happier than I had ever known him.

Mike and Shelly's family were almost grown, and true to their teachings, were community minded and active in our work. James and Marion had returned to their home, it was well built and suitable for the conditions we were experiencing. James had taken over a lot of my duties, I was experiencing the early symptoms of aging. It happens to all of us.

I spent most of my time trying to look into the future and plan for growth. Brian and Danny, both very educated men, were my right arms. They seemed to be able to read the changes in the environment as if they had experienced it before. We had made trips to the libraries and retrieved hundreds of books of all kinds.

My interests lay in history, psychology, and law, and anything else that had to do with human behavior. We had a few behavioral incidents through the years. We had no means of incarceration. We had decided that our ideas on crime and punishment must be new and innovative. We decided that, although we hated the idea, we must be willing to adapt capitol punishment to fit our laws. But, it would be used only in the most extreme of cases.

We had arrived at a time when, if someone would not accept our law, then banishment would be the most acceptable of punishment. But for the most part, minor infractions would be countered with community service details, or exclusion from social activities.

We had not had to use these new laws very much. A couple of times at Rustic, and Max in his community in Wyoming, had some newcomers that had not wanted to comply. They were sent packing. But as yet, no extreme violence of any kind.

That is, until June of '31. We allowed two new people to join at Rustic. They seemed like nice people. They worked for a few weeks. Early one morning they were seen coming out of a cabin that didn't belong to them. A little later that day the alarm was raised. A friend going to check on the young couple that lived there found them both dead, stabbed repeatedly.

David found the couple sneaking down river and arrested them, bringing them back at gunpoint. We buried the couple and after a couple of days we convened the council. I sat as spokesman, and brought the proceedings to order.

"Ladies and Gentlemen, we have convened this council to determine the case of Greg and Penny Marshall regarding the deaths of Sharon and Steve Hempstead. Would the council for prosecution please state your case."

The prosecutor, Evan McGregor, rose to his feet. He had studied some law at University of Wyoming.

"Your Honors, it is of our opinion that the plaintiffs did willfully murder the Hempstead couple and we will attempt to outline that in due course. Thank you."

"Will council for the defense please make your opening statement."

The defense council, Steve Schmidt, had also studied at the University of Wyoming and had indeed been classmates of Evan. He rose and faced the court.

"Your Honors, the defendants plead not guilty of murder. They say they were attacked by the other couple and merely defended themselves. We plan to outline this, in due course."

As the prosecutor began his case, I found myself immersed in the proceedings. I listened intently, as each detail was given, the times that each occurrence took place. The gist of it was, that the couple had gone to the dead couples cabin, and in the course of the evenings social activity the young man who was now dead had been too forward and had made a pass at Penny, which she declined. He became incensed about it and had caused a scene, which turned to a fight. Steve had picked up a poker from the fireplace and attempted to hit Greg. As he did, Penny stabbed him with the butcher knife. Then Sharon attacked Penny, and Greg, trying to defend Penny, struggle with Sharon and she was killed with her own knife by accident. At least this what the defense claimed. After the prosecution made their case, I asked David Suttle to come forth.

"David, you saw the bodies and the crime scene. You have experienced first hand, hand to hand fighting with knives as a part of your military service. Would you tell the council your interpretation of the events in that cabin? And outline why you think it happened that way."

David rose to speak, "Members of the Council. As Head of Security I was called to that cabin on the morning when the bodies were found. I entered and found the couples bodies on opposite sides of the room. I first examined Steve's body. As you know, Steve was a big man, six foot two at least. Steve had a knife wound entering his back just to the left of his spine going in and hitting his heart and lungs. There were no signs of a struggle. Furniture was all upright, except for a small table Steve took with him when he fell. Your Honors, Penny is five foot two or three. It would have been impossible for Penny to have delivered that fatal thrust from that angle at that height. Also, Sharon was killed from a knife penetration from behind, inflicted around her body from the left side entering her heart, very unlikely to be done from a struggle from a man much taller than herself in a struggle. Also, there was no indication of a struggle. Clothes were not in disarray. Also, Penny is left handed. It would have fit the wound exactly. It is my opinion that it was murder, not self defense. Although, I do not have a motive. The Hempsteads had very few belongings or possessions."

David returned to his seat. As I shifted my gaze, I became aware of that the Marshall's were glaring at him, as if they could do the same to him as they had been accused of doing to the couple.

We adjourned to deliberate. It required no discussion. We returned to the floor with an unanimous verdict. Murder.

I took a bit longer to arrive at sentencing. But we agreed that it would be death for both. The following morning they were hanged from a cottonwood tree along the river. Death should not be a spectator sport. We had chosen designated witnesses' to document the execustion, and they were the only ones allowed to be present. Thus was our first large offense against members of our community conducted.

At that point we decided we were going to do a three person interview system be for people were to be admitted to any of our communities. Each interview to be held and recorded separately and with different interviewers. We just had too much to risk. It sounds prejudicial and it reeks of profiling, but the fact that people coming in from that devastated outside world where surviving could have been animalistic, were questionable. We had to be sure.

At our monthly meeting the first Sunday of July, the question came up. A young man in his late twenties stood.

"I have to ask. Why are we gutting buildings and building new ones? It is a lot of work. There are lots of nice homes in Fort Collins that are still intact. Why can't we move there?"

I stood, "I apologize for not doing this earlier, but here goes." I looked at the young man addressing the council.

"First of all, this is a free society, and if you wish, you may go right down there and move in and avoid all this hard work. But, when you get ready to go to the bathroom, you are going to find that the toilet won't flush, because there is no water. And if it did, pretty soon you would be up to your elbows in pooh, cause there is no sewer system working. Then, you will want to fix yourself some food. Oops again. No water. Then you will try to have some more light. Wow, no way of lighting your house. No electricity, no gas to heat with. These houses were built with central heat, so no way to warm it.

"You see, all these cities are built on a really fragile grid. That grid is no more. To adapt them to our needs would be futile, that is why we had to start new communities. And as we go, we have to be wary of being sucked back onto another grid at sometime. We need each home and business to be energy sustainable, and able to stand on its own feet.

"Many years ago I read a story about some old wise men in India that went around advising the people, who at that time, lived in family units, but in individual houses. One day, they came to visit their people and found they had all moved together into villages. They were horrified. They thought this would be the end of civilization and mankind. Well, it may have taken a few thousand years but it finally almost ended. I am not saying that small villages are bad, but we should shun the ideas of cities anymore. It is my belief."

The young man looked at me, "Thank you, sir, you are right. I appreciate the explanation."

I looked around. "Iif you have questions about why we do things, come ask us. Don't let doubts create dissension. Even if you think we are wrong, come talk about it. Unity is our strength!"

Our communities thrived for the next several years. The winters were still bad, but we were getting longer growing seasons, and the greenhouse construction continued. We now had five along the north side of the Poudre River below Rustic. We had increased our livestock, and in turn tripled our pastureland. The Wyoming community had been harder hit by the cold, but had managed to stay on a positive growth schedule. I had spent all my spare time trying to develop a radio system and expand our communications with other areas.

In the spring of '35, one morning in April, Nell and I awoke. Amigo was laying between our feet, his favorite place for sleeping. He had gotten old, this morning in particular, he didn't seem to want to get up, we turned around, and lay on each side of him. He raised his head and nosed Nell on the cheek and licked her face softly, then turned his head and did the same for me. He looked me very intently in the eyes for a few seconds, his tail thumped a couple of times. He lay his head back and sighed a big sigh. His breathing slowed then quit. He had been waiting for his two people to awake to say his last goodbye. We lay for an hour or more, crying and holding him. That afternoon we went out to his favorite points along the rim of the canyon and dug him a grave. We wrapped him in his favorite blanket and laid him quietly to rest. He would never be forgotten, and we could visit him often.

May 1, 2035

I was scanning frequencies. I picked up a few words. I answered. No one came back, I was sure I had heard the transmission on this frequency. I waited. Two hours pasted, then three. I put down the book I was reading. I called for Nell.

She came out, " Yes Dear?"

"Would you stay here and listen to the radio for a minute? I need to go to the bathroom."

"Of course."

I went in the house and had just finished my duties in the bathroom when heard Nell call.

"Jeff!"

I jumped and ran. I entered the radio room in time to see Nell key the mike and say, "Please stand by."

Another voice answered, "Roger, will do."

She got up and I sat down. "This is Fortress 1,

over."

"Roger, Fortress. this Rendezvous City, come in."

"Roger Rendezvous. What is your 20, over?"

"About 30 miles west of Flagstaff, Arizona. And yours, over?"

"We are about twenty miles northwest of Fort Collins, Colorado. Rendezvous, what is your condition, over?"

"Oh, we are doing fine, Fortress, thanks for asking. We had a few rough years, but have survived. yourself, over?"

"Likewise, and thanks for asking as well. Any news from the outside world, over?"

"Yes. We are in contact with a station in California. Seems like oceans all over the globe are rising drastically. They say their seismic activities have increased since the oceans have come up. It seems that most of the southern half of America is sinking or at least going under. Same place the great inland seas of prehistoric times were. It is really bazaar, I guess most of Texas is underwater now. Over."

I heard Nell gasp. I needed time to digest all this.

"Roger that, Rendezvous. I need to tell our other two communities this news." I told him what our other frequencies were and when we monitored them. He gave us his times, and we signed off.

"Shit, what next?" I went inside, Nell was wiping her eyes. She echoed me, "What next?"

"The planet is alive, my dear, and she is changing her dress!"

I went to visit Brian and Danny. I sat down and

related my conversation with the Arizona community.

Brian was the first to answer, "Jeff, I am not surprised. I am surprised at the speed in which it has happened, and a bit surprised with it happening with the winters we had. However, it won't stop very fast, you can expect it to go on for a while, and it won't recede for a very, very long time. I don't know what will happen next."

Danny interjected, "I do. California is going under, probably soon. The pressure of rising oceans is going to put too much pressure on the San Andreas fault. Expect a big one."

I said thanks, and asked them to contact Max and Chuck and fill them in on the news. I went down to James and Mike's homes and filled everyone in and called a meeting for the next week at Rustic.

May 26, 2035
The day dawned bright and clear. We had

ridden in the evening before. It was good seeing all our friends. Rustic was a town reborn. The morning sun glistened on the greenhouse glass backed into the rocky hill side above the Poudre River. The river itself had began running strong earlier than usual. The runoff being early, I hoped we wouldn't go back into another heat wave, as we did in '22. Time would tell.

We visited the greenhouses. Nell and Marion had taught the managers well. The view to the river thru the glass made me think of some giant star ship approaching it's landing on the river. In another month the root crops would be planted in fields along the river, all the way down to Ted's Place on US 287.

As the morning passed the time for the meeting approached. I realized that I hadn't seen Nell in awhile. I walked to where the old store had been. It was now our commissary, as well as the Lodge there. The entrepreneurial nature of our community had risen to a perfectly delightful level. The commissary was filled with food items, hand made tools, crafts, clothing.

and many ,many, other items. All created by the very people that used them. There were many other items we still needed. We had people that could have risen to the task, but lack of raw materials was the problem. For instance, saddles, tack, harness'. We had no leather, and no tannery. But we were working on the problem. We had cleaned out all the Western Stores and Saddleries in the area, but it still wasn't enough, and our horse population was growing every year.

Every time we had gone to Fort Collins I was amazed at the changes. The once busy little city was falling into ruin. The plains were reclaiming it. Everywhere there was a crack in the pavement or sidewalk, a weed or grass was growing. The buildings were home now to the various critters of the region, but not for long. Without attention, the weather was claiming them. Yet Nell and I had ridden by the old log cabin in downtown La Porte that was built in 1836 or so, and it appeared unchanged.

But this day we had to tell our populace more

news, and guess what? That obligation fell to me.

I was introduced by Mike McCollum. I rose and approached the podium, to a bit of applause.

"Thanks, Mike for that wonderful introduction. I see folks here that I haven't had the pleasure of an introduction. We can remedy that later and please come and tell me about yourselves. We want to thank Max, and the Wyoming community that came with him. I see lots of new babies out there. Someone has been busy." There was some laughter.

"My first duty here is to offer some appreciation and praise for those that serve the public. First of all comes Shelly McCullom, our Head of Education. She has informed me that she has taken our level up to completion of High School, with five graduates this year, all with high grades and honors. Shelly, you and those five please stand and take a bow."

Shelly and her students got a huge round of applause.

"Next, is my life companion Nell. And Marion Roberts and her managers in the greenhouses. They are taking our food production to above acceptable levels. Thank you for your service." There was another round of applause.

"Next comes David Suttle and our security force. They have kept a large body of people safe for quite a while, even under horrible conditions. David." Another round of applause.

"Our construction crews headed by Arne, James Roberts, and their numerous foremen. They can handle any task great or small, we owe you." More applause.

"Finally, our Council. Folks, I would never believe that twelve people could literally be of one mind and could work together that way. Some of us are getting on in years, and the torch is going to be passed to you. With that responsibility, I can only hope, you will be able to attain that selflessness that becomes great leaders. You know who they are. Take today and go find them and shake their hand and tell them how much you appreciate them. They held your lives and the lives of your families in their hands with their decisions and wisdom.

"Next item of business is both exciting and foreboding. A few days ago I received a radio call from a colony in the mountains of Arizona, near Flagstaff. People much like ourselves, they withstood the trials of the chaotic years, and have survived and are now doing well. I have spoken to them and they have talents and commodities that would be of value to us, as we have for them. At some time we may try to establish trade with them, but that will come much later. What they have brought us is news of the outside world. Some of which may be disturbing. You should prepare yourselves for this.

"I have learned that the oceans all around the planet are rising. Our experts expect this to continue for sometime. This should not worry you for yourselves, we are safe. It seems that much of the southern U.S. seems to be sinking, or at least being covered with water. As some of you know, this is not the first time this has happened. It happened anciently. A good part of our country was once an inland sea. It appears, that is becoming that again. No one seems to know how long it will be that way. Texas is mostly underwater now." There were *Oh*'s and gasps from the audience. "Also, the rising seas seem to be creating seismic disturbances in California. Our scientists believe that soon a major earthquake will greatly damage it. The seas have traveled up through the Baja Peninsula. The Gulf of California and the valleys up as far as Yuma are now under water. All we can do is wait and see.

"I guess, for now, that is enough food for thought. So if there is no other business, we will adjourn and let the festivities begin!"

That afternoon, I was asked to perform three marriages, one of my most happy of chores.

I sat down at one of the tables with Nell and Dave and Sam Love and others to have lunch Dave S. and James and Arne sat across from me.

Dave S. spoke, "Jeff, while the weather is nice, we would like to take a journey to Denver and maybe Colorado Springs to scout for more communities and things we can use. We would like two wagon teams and ten riders, and weapons and supplies. Do you approve?"

"Of course I approve. I have been thinking of expanding our borders for some time. We need to grow to survive. Talk to Chuck and Max while everyone is here. You can ask for volunteers. Choose your people carefully, but I don't have to tell you that. I think you should have a larger party though."

"You may be right. Thanks, we will organize it."

We had an awesome evening, music and

dancing under the stars. But Nell seemed preoccupied and not her normal playful, happy self.

We left early next morning for The Fortress. James and Marion and Mike and Shelly rode with us. Nell and Marion spent most of the day talking to each other. Upon arrival at The Fortress, Brian and Danny had dinner prepared for us. So we ate and the two couples prepared to depart to their own houses. Marion hugged Nell, and I noticed tears in her eyes.

After they had gone and dinner put away, Brian and Danny retired to their own quarters. We showered and lay in bed together. I was sixty-seven now, Nell was fifty six. And although the fires that had united us were banked somewhat, the desire for closeness never abated. As we lay in each others arms now I felt just as much in love now as I did in 2001.

"Nell, we have been together now for thirty-four years, and I know when you are troubled, and I know something is wrong now. Will you please tell me?"

Tears came to her eyes. "I have been dreading this for some time, this not easy. I have talked to Marion and Shelly and Dakota and Diane. There is only one answer. Here, put your hand here."

She guided my hand to her left breast and placed it on it, telling me to feel inside. I immediately could feel a large mass.

"Oh my God, Nell! How long have you known?"

"Sometime now. I haven't wanted to burden you with it. You have had your hands full. Without the medical technology that we have lost, there is nothing that could be done anyway."

I held her in my arms for the next few hours. Not since Amigo had passed had I felt such sorrow. Now it was not just sorrow, it felt the first real fear I had experienced since '22. Sleep came only sporadically all that night. *Oh my poor Nell!*

They say that most people never realize the value of something until they have lost it. I hadn't lost Nell yet, but believe me, I knew her value. She was my rock, she kept me balanced. A true Libra, she appreciated beauty and sought order. She abhorred violence, but was ready always to defend those who needed defending.

I laughed to myself while remembering an event in Austin. We were staying one weekend at an event in Austin at an apartment belonging to a friend of hers named Mark. Mark was a gay man and had a boyfriend, a part time live-in boyfriend who was fairly obnoxious. Mark was away, and we were sleeping in Marks bedroom when we awoke in the middle of the night to find the boyfriend in the bedroom going through Mark's stuff. Nell was out of the bed in a second, butt naked. She put the boyfriend out of the bedroom, down the hall and out the door and told him to not come back until Mark came home. He didn't either.

Without the benefit of what had been modern day medicine, the prognosis for her wasn't good. I knew that unless something happened like a miracle, she would need lots of care and painkiller on down the line. Later that day I got on the radio and spoke to the leaders of all communities and asked them to be on the lookout for any medicines of the opiate type they might know of, and also, to not spread this news around.

I had decided to make myself more available to her and to turn over most of my duties to the Council. I announced that decision at our next monthly meeting in June.

Nell and I spent our summer doing what young lovers do best. We went to the waterfall on warm days and took showers in the cold water. We rode our horses, finding trails that would take us to beautiful places in the forest. One day, we had tied our horses and climbed up to one of the rock towers that boasted a long bench seat of rock, with a view of the great plains to the east of us. The afternoon sun cast long shadows out from us, a peaceful serene setting. She looked up at me.

"Jeff, thank you for giving me this beautiful life. You know if we hadn't met at TRF, I might never have known this beautiful place. You have been a constant companion, yet you have given me the freedom to be me. I am so grateful for my life. I have learned more than I ever dreamed I would learn, and yet haven't touched all the things I would like to know. I have met the greatest friends I could have ever dreamed to meet. Almost ever day of my life, it has been to wake up next to you, and smell your smell, and feel your warmth. I don't know how long I will live, but I will never be happier than I am. I don't feel cheated by this, I guess I spent to much time with Chris and his influence to feel cheated. You should know, though, that you have made me happy."

I couldn't speak. I simply held her in my arms, and choked back the tears.

We stayed busy, Nell and I. We visited all the

communities over the summer months, playing with the children. We decided they were all ours. We had not had any ourselves. We didn't know why, we just didn't. So we played with them and we spoiled them like grandparents are supposed to. We went to the schools and told stories of the days past. I told stories of the Great Wars our great and even farther back great-grandfathers had fought in, and encouraged them when they grew up to remember them and not fall victims to those mistakes again. We would sit around the campfires and answer questions from the eleven and twelve year olds that had never know any other kind of life.

"Grampa Jeff, I have read stories of tall buildings that had elevators that take you the tops of them in a minute. Is that true?"

"Yes, that's true. In some of the big cities that were destroyed by the storms some of them were a hundred stories tall."

The questions would go on into the night,

until mothers would come and take sleepy-eyed but still curious children away to their beds.

David and his crew made their four week trip to Denver and Colorado Springs. They came back with many things to aid us in our building projects. They also found two more communities south of us. One, living near Nederland, and one in the mountains of the Rampart Range near Colorado Springs. The military bases had been abandoned, no sign of anyone there anymore. But it all seemed safe. No violence left, no hostile people, indeed it seemed as if they had - to use an old term from early in the century - been 'scared straight'. The common attitude seemed to be that violence and disorder simply didn't work.

With that in mind, Nell and I approached the Council with an idea. We wanted to take all the kids from our communities on a 2 day field trip to Fort Collins so that they could see firsthand what civilization had looked like. The idea was approved, and we were to meet at Rustic on July 28, this being the year 2035, thirteen years since the Great Chaos had come upon us. We would go prepared with riders with arms, just for safeties sake and would take four days worth of food.

The morning of the 28th came and four wagon loads of children of all ages and their parents, with twelve outriders for escort rolled down the road from Rustic. Everyone was excited. Down the road, past the old tunnel and past the old club that was called Mishawaka's, past the where the community that was called Poudre Park. We actually had a small satellite community there, and two greenhouses. There was also room for gardens there. We picked up four more kids and their mom's. At an abandoned recreational spot along the Poudre we pitched a camp for the night. Everyone was tired, so we all slept well.

Next morning we arose and set out early. We came out of the hills just before Ted's Place. A great exclamation came up from the kids. It was open country. They had never been out of the mountains. We followed old US 287 through the little town of La Porte. We stopped and showed them the old log cabin there. They weren't nearly as excited with it as all the modern buildings laying in ruins. We continued our drive down into Fort Collins, through the 'Old Town' district along College Avenue, the horses feet clippity-clopping down the pavement. When we reached the Campus at CSU, we stopped and set up camp at on the grounds. Plenty of grazing for the animals and a great place to have a bonfire and talk about this great institute of learning. Two of the moms, both teachers, and Shelly McCullom took a troop of the students and went for a walk around the Campus. The moms had been students here years ago, and were able to point out key spots and relate the activities that took place there.

The city I remembered had taken on the look I remembered from the TV show in the early 2000's. Weeds and grass grew out of the streets and sidewalks. Across the street stood a small yellow building, the sign read 'Mellow Yellow'. I wondered.

I yelled, "David, come walk with me!"

David turned and we walked across the four lane street. The little building was still locked up. We kicked the door in. Evidently vandals, (not to say that we weren't at the moment) had gotten in previously, but there were still pipes and bongs and magazines and all sorts of goods, none of which were edible. We filled a couple of boxes and carried them away with us, vowing to tell the other adults about the little 'Head Shop' from the past.

That night we built our fire and roasted deer and elk sausages over it and we ate melons and fruit. We told stories about the life on this street, about the automobiles that filled it all day and most of the night, about the crowds of young people that had sat and conversed and sang songs and talked about art and philosophy, and what they were going to do in the future. Some of the kids wanted to know what the three-eyed boxes hang on wire in the middle of the streets were for. We explained they were stop and go lights for the cars. Then they wanted to know why that was necessary. When we explained that there was so many cars it was necessary to be able to control them, they just couldn't believe it, and discussed it for some time afterward.

It had gotten late when we noticed the eyes in the darkness. Dogs. Dogs whose parents had at one time lived in the houses, but were now gone. Dogs that were survivors. We knew that many of them had been eaten, but some had survived, and had reverted back to their ancestral roles. We decided to keep the fires burning all night and children would sleep in the wagons. Several guards would be posted around our perimeter.

David said, "You never see them in the day time. They have reverted back to there nocturnal selves. We saw them in Denver and The Springs, but not so many as this."

When morning came, we were alone once again. I wondered if they were just curious about these two legged creatures, and if their

DNA told them they should come join us. Or if they smelled food. That thought was a bit scary.

The next day we toured the city. We stopped at the Poudre Valley Hospital, and we explained to the students what it's purpose was. We sent a scrounging crew inside. They came back with several different types of medications, no way of know if they were still good. One of the items was a container of morpheme ampules. I knew that they had been carried into battle during our wars. I packed them carefully. I would check with people that were more knowledgeable when we got back to our civilization. Having seen and talked about many things by now ot was mid-afternoon so we headed back up toward our canyon. Just north of Fort Collins is a large cement plant. We had stopped on the side of the road, explaining to the kids what it was when the thought hit me.

"David, has anyone ever checked that out to see if there is usable cement there?"

"Way ahead of you boss. C'mon Arne, we will

catch up with you in a while." They turned their horses and loped off toward the big plant.

We followed US 287 back around to Highway 14. As we turned at Ted's Place, about a dozen riders came out from under the trees beside the old store. At first I thought it might riders from Rustic come to escort us home. Then I realized, these men were dressed like the Native Americans of the 1880's. They approached us cautiously. We pulled up and stopped. They approached us and stopped. One of the men slid off his horse and walked to my wagon. I handed the reins to Nell and stepped off to meet him. He appeared in his forties, quite fit, his hair long and braided. He stuck out his hand, which I took.

"Hello, I am John Willow Tree."

"Hi, I am Jeff Bartlett."

"Me and my friends are Arapahoe from the Wind River Reservation up north in Wyoming. We are down here scouting our ancient homelands."

"We have some colonies up river here aways." About that time, David and Arne came riding up. David dismounted and joined me.

"This is David Suttle. He is our Chief of Security." About that time, a shout from one of the other men.

"David!"

One of the young Native American men jumped from his horse and literally pounced on David. The action took me and John Willow Tree totally aback.

David yelled back, "Mike! You son of a bitch! I didn't think I would ever see you again!"

The two men hugged each other and wrestled for a minute. Upon seeing the startled looks on our faces, they turned and David explained.

"Jeff, this is Michael Grey Fox. He served with me in Afghanistan. He saved my life a couple of times!"

"And you did the same for me, brother," Mike retorted.

I turned to John and said, "Would you men like to follow us up to our community and rest for a couple of days and see if we have anything we can help each other out?"

"We would be proud to visit your home. Besides, I don't think it is fair to separate these two so soon after they have been united again."

"Alright, then lets get these kids home before too late."

As we traveled, John and I talked. I told him about the small hog back that was just below the place where we met. It was cut off by the river eons ago. I told him that the Arapahoe had considered it a ceremonial place. The Bonner

Home had sat just below it, and Jim Bonner had endeavored to keep people off it. John said on his way out he would go there. He might well be the first of his tribe to visit it in a hundred fifty years or more. He thanked me and said, "It is a good thing that we met."

David and Mike rode together all the way to Rustic. We could hear them laughing and talking, just like the brothers they were. It was late night, indeed early morning, as we had to stop and rest the teams several times in their steady climb up the canyon, when we finally arrived. Willing hands lifted sleeping children wrapped in blankets against the evening chill, and took them to beds. Other hands took harness' from horses, and took them to stables to be rubbed down and fed. I felt the need for some of those willing hands myself. My old bones ached, and as I looked at Nell, I realized she was exhausted. I took her to our room and put her to bed. She turned over and murmured, "Thank you," and was lost in dreamland. The Arapahoe men were sent to our bunkhouse, their horses taken care of for them. Food was brought I. I sat for a short while, everyone had so many questions for our guests.

I finally told everyone to go to bed, the question could wait for tomorrow. Our guests had just made a long ride.

Next morning a scrumptious breakfast was served. It took us years to get chickens started so that we could have eggs, and on occasion, chicken. It always made my day to sit down and see two eggs staring back at me. This day was no different. John looked across the table from in front of me. "You people eat good!"

I looked at him, "It wasn't always so, John."

"I have no doubt. A lot of my people died the first three years."

After breakfast we walked out to our outside meeting area. A crowd had already gathered. We sat down at the tables, and I had Shelly and the teachers describe our trip in detail. We decided it was a total success. A lot of questions were answered that were difficult to just explain, but when seen were more satisfying.

Then, we gave John Willow Tree the floor. He rose and introduced the members of his party. He explained that they were members of the Northern Arapahoe tribe, that all this front range and more had been their ancient lands. Several of the hills in our area still held their medicine wheels. He went on to say that they, too, had suffered in the years after Chaos, but were becoming strong. He ended by saying they would be happy to answer questions. He allowed that he was not used to speaking and was sure he had left out many things.

The first question was a good one. A teenage girl asked, "Have you seen many other people? Is it true, that most people are dead?"

His answer excited me.

"Yes, there are people still living. The cities are

all empty, but small communities still live here and there. Like you, although, you are an exception. You are much better off than most. You should be proud of your leaders, they have done well."

Next question, a young man asks, "You say this was once your land. Are you planning on claiming it again?"

John smiled, "No, the Arapahoe and most of the people you refer to as the 'Native Americans' did not believe that land should be owned. We believe that we have a stewardship to protect it. We shared it with other tribes as hunting grounds. But we asked for it to be respected. It was a gift from our god, The Great Spirit. We still feel that way."

Another question, "What would you like to trade with us?"

"Oh, many things. We have kept knowledge of healing plants. We have vegetables we would share seeds with you. We have horses. We see you have some, we have many. We would herd some buffalo down here so they could grow and multiply. We have skills that your people have forgotten. We could teach you. Looking around, you have many things we would love to be able to utilize. For one, your greenhouses. Some of your technology would be most welcome."

The meeting turned into a buzz of discussions as people turned to the young men and started talking with them. It did me good to see our community so animated.

Idaho

Damien had just walked out on the deck when the earth began to move and shake. *Oh my God, it's Rainier!* He thought. He looked to the west. No cloud. Surely he would be able to see it from here. Sandy was beside him in a few seconds.

"Damien, what is it?"

"I am not sure, maybe Rainier. I can't tell."

Russ came running from his house, with Misty close behind.

"Dad, the Caldera, at Yellowstone, it's erupting!"

"Oh Shit! I hope Rainier doesn't follow suit. We are in a bad place if it does."

"We may be anyway, according to reports I have read."

The next few weeks were full of fear and frustration for the people near Coeur d' Alene. But gradually the eruption subsided.

About a month later, Damien was sitting on the deck and Russ came trotting across from his cabin.

"Dad, I have the answer. I know how to move the people and a great bit of our possessions."

"OK, tell me," Damien answered.

"By railroad," Russ answered with a grin.

"Well, have you been hiding a train engine all this time without telling me?"

"No, I was going through some old history books. Look here." He took out a picture. It was a horse drawn trolly in New York City in the early 1900's.

"We can build wagons and take the wheels and axles off those trucks and vans down at the railroad yard and mount them on the wagons. The grades will be slighter. It should be easier than just trying to do it by wagon."

"By God, Russ, it might just work. Let's saddle up and go see Ed Brawner. He used to work for the railroad."

"I am on my way!"

They saddled quickly, and half an hour later were riding up to Ed's house across the valley. Ed met them at the door and invited them in. As they explained their plan, he sat up in his chair and slapped his knees.

"You betcha! It will work! In fact, we might even have some wagons down at the old yard that could be rebuilt. I'm with ya. This the best idea yet. And, by the way, there is a line that runs outta here down through Helena, Montana all the way to Cheyenne, Wyoming, and farther."

Ed stepped into the next room and returned with a bottle of Jack Daniels about three quarter gone.

"Here I have been saving this for an important occasion for years now. This is an important occasion."

He poured three shots and they toasted their new adventure.

They worked for over a year, building the wagons. They traded for horses, even found some big drafts. In the fall of '41, they were ready, but it was too late in the season. They needed to wait until spring, at least April, maybe May.

The months dragged by. But it couldn't be helped. They were planning on transporting a hundred men, women, and children across over a thousand miles of they didn't know what. In April they started hauling possessions and goods to the railroad yards. By the first of May they were ready to go. Russ and Damien had taken all of their wind generators, batteries, water turbines, research materials, even their old computers, their food staples, everything. They had four railroad cars, covered, fifty head of horses, plus what the outriders were riding.

On the morning of May 5th, 2042, they headed out down the right of way. They had rigged teams of three in line to pull the railway wagons. The wagons were equipped with braking mechanisms. It all worked, and they were on their way on a bright sunshiny morning.

ಐ

And so it went the next year or so. We built, we educated, we traded, we innovated. Our Arapahoe neighbors to the north contributed a huge herd of horses, something for our young men and women to develop skills for. They all had to be trained. The last week of October after we had first met, John and about twenty-five of his tribesmen appeared late one evening. We shook hands and sat to eat a meal together.

"Jeff, we have over a hundred head of buffalo tucked into the little valley just to the north of where the river comes out of the canyon. It is getting late, they will stay close for shelter during the winter. There is much forage there. The buffalo in Wyoming are becoming like they were in the old days, and the wolves are getting thick as well. They have no natural enemies, but you should freely begin to hunt them. They will provide plenty of meat for your people. Don't waste anything. Use their hides and all parts. They are a gift from the Great Spirit."

We did as he said, and shared with the other communities as well. We traded with the new communities near Boulder and Colorado Springs, and within the next two years had a regular trade route with wagons, and even a stagecoach.

In 2038 we were awakened one morning with a shudder. It almost felt like the earth had quit turning for a moment. Then another, then another. We went running out of the cabin, looking to see if we could see what was going on. Dave Love and Sam, were standing on the deck, clutching their robes. Brian and Danny came out of the radio shack.

"Jeff," said Danny, "California is gone. They had the big one. We just got a short bit before their station went dead. The station in Williams, Arizona said, from what they understood, the whole fault has ruptured!"

Brian answered, "Well, it was due to be in Alaska in about a million years ago anyway. Now it won't be late!" He looked around at everyone looking at him. "I'm sorry, I realize it is a tremendous lose of life and resources. But after a while I guess you just get numb to it. What can happen next?"

Dave answered, "Please don't ask!"

Danny turned back to the radio room, "I am going to pass the word to the other communities that maybe didn't receive the message."

I turned to go back inside and noticed Nell was missing. I went back and found her in the bedroom, looking quite ill. She had steadily been getting weaker over the last six months. I did everything I knew to do to make her life easy. John had brought some native medicines with him for her, but nothing seemed to help. It wasn't so much the pain, but just weakness and constantly ill. Her beautiful blonde hair had turned grey, and she had lost considerable weight. But when I looked at her I still saw the beautiful blonde girl at the drum jam so long ago. I would go to bed at night and hold her in my arms if she was feeling well. Sometimes, I think she said she was feeling ok when she wasn't.

I spent the day sitting and reading to her. She enjoyed the papers that the Old Man had written. She said they made her see life differently than she had expected as a young girl growing up in Texas.

Late in the afternoon, James and Marion came to visit. I left Nell in her capable hands, and joined James on the deck.

"James, I don't think she has much longer." I choked out. "I don't want to see her pass, but it is killing me inside to see her suffer this way."

James put his hand on my shoulder, "Yeah, I know, Jeff. We all love her. Not like you, but she has brought beauty into all our lives. She has touched everyone." He paused. "I am pretty sure you know that she and Marion had a love affair going on for years. Marion doesn't think I know, but it was real evident. And I didn't object at all," he laughed, "I fell in love with her the first time I ever saw her that day she was making snow angels in the nude. She was so embarrassed."

I laughed, "Yes, she was. And yes, I knew about her and Marion. I caught them one day at the waterfall."

We sat and talked till it was getting dark. I think I was first to notice a glow to the north just a little west of north.

"Look, James. What is that?"

"I don't know. A forest fire maybe?"

It was then that Mike's son, Chase, who had been taking a shift on the radio, came running out.

"Uncle Jeff, the Yellowstone Caldera is erupting! The Arapahoes are coming south, all of them. they are asking for help."

"Get a message back, we are on our way. And alert Max. We need empty wagons and fresh horses and extra teams."

James said, "I am on my way. I will get my two teams and wagon and head out tonight."

"Be careful, James. The scientists said this thing is capable of taking out half of North America."

He nodded and went inside and told Marion to stay with Nell and help me. As we came out, Chase said, "I am going with James. Tell Mom and Dad."

I nodded. He had grown into a fine young man. I knew Mike would be worried, but proud of him.

I had thought of going with James myself. Then I realized I was looking out with the eyes of a thirty year old that were imprisoned in a body of a man pushing seventy. I thought better of it. They will be hurrying to meet the Arapahoe, I might hold them up.

All night long the sky glowed, the next

morning, a pillar of smoke. *My God! Is the earth trying to destroy itself, and all it's people?* I suppose I couldn't blame her. For decades we had raped and pillaged her, and then did our best to destroy her and all her resources. I sat on the deck and watched and waited. It would be days before we would know the fate of our Arapahoe friends.

It was a nice day, so we carried Nell out on the deck and made her comfortable. Marion fixed her a soup made from buffalo tongue with herbs and vegetables. It smelled divine and so I had a bit with her. She laughed when I told her it was really good, but not as good as her tongue used to be. She punched my leg and said, "You need to find your self another tongue." I put my arm around her and told her that a page had been turned in my life, and that wasn't on this new page and she needn't concern herself. She squeezed my leg, saying, "Jeff Bartlett, I love you." A single tear ran down her cheek.

She looked up at the distant smoke. "Jeff, are they going to be alright? Are we going to be alright?"

"Time will tell, sweetheart, time will tell. We have survived some awful things and we are still here. We just keep on moving forward, it is only thing we can do." I gripped her hand, "You just concern your self with taking care of my favorite girlfriend."

'

"You have got another one," she giggled.

"Aww, I outta spank you," I laughed, "but you would probably like that."

"OHHH Baby! Come on!"

As the afternoons in Colorado often do, it clouded and a chill came over the mountain. We moved Nell back inside.

She smiled as we lay her back in bed. She said, "This has just been the best afternoon, you guys! Lay down with me a minute or so."

We did, Marion on one side, myself on the other. We lay for a short while cuddling her close, her eyes closed and her voice trailed off.

"Oh, my lovers, I so love both of you. Thank you for making my life so grand."
She was asleep.

As we got up, my eyes met Marion's. We stood up and hugged each other.

"Jeff, I can never thank you enough for sharing her with me."

"And I can never thank you enough for loving her."

It was over a week, before the first wagons came from the north. Wagons loaded with women children, possessions, goods, food stuffs. Horses pulling travois', people walking beside them. There must of been two hundred or more. As a wagon arrived it would unload and a fresh team hitched and it would head back, for all that month it continued. When finally they had all arrived, there we close to five hundred.

John and I met with the leaders of the communities, we expressed our sorrow that they had been forced to leave their homes. But on the bright side, now we could work together much easier. It was agreed that sometimes when a door closes, another better one opens.

November 25, 2038

It was Thanksgiving Day, 2038. We had occasion for thanksgiving that year. The smoke from Yellowstone had gone away, and the Caldera slumbered once more. We had gathered our friends on our mountain top. We had a lavish meal and good music and story telling. A young Arapahoe girl, one of John's granddaughters, gathered the little children around her and told them the story of Spider, the Trickster.

Nihancan and the Dwarf's Arrow

Nihancan the Spider was out traveling in

search of some mischief he could do to please himself. Along a creek he found a patch of sweet berries, and while he was eating them he heard the sound of someone cutting wood. The sound seemed to come from a grove of cotton woods across the creek. "I must go over there," Nihancan said to himself, "I have heard that dwarfs who make wonderful arrows live in that place. It is time that I played a trick on them."

He crossed a stream and among the cotton woods he found a dwarf making an arrow out of an immense tree that had been cut down.

"Well, little brother," said Nihancan, "what are you making?"

"You have eyes to see," replied the dwarf, who continued shaping the tree into an arrow as long as ten men and as thick as a man's body.

"I have heard about your ability to shoot very large arrows," Nihancan said. "But surely you do not expect me to believe that so small a person as you can lift so large a tree. Let me see you shoot it. I will stand over there against that hillside and you can shoot at me."

"I do not want to do that, Nihancan," the dwarf answered, "for I might kill you."

At that, Nihancan laughed and began taunting the dwarf, who remained silent until Nihancan said scornfully, "Just as I thought, you are unable to lift the arrow, and so cannot shoot at me. I shall go on my way.

Then the dwarf said, "I will shoot." Nihancan went toward the hillside and asked in a mocking voice, "Shall I stand here?"

"No, farther away," said the dwarf. "You might get hurt there."

Nihancan went on, and asked again, "Shall I stand here?" But the dwarf continued to tell him to go farther off. At last Nihancan called out, "I will not go any farther. I am as far as your voice reaches." He was now on the hillside, and as he turned to look back he was astonished to see the dwarf pick up the huge tree with one hand.

At once he became frightened and shouted, "Don't shoot at me, little brother. I know you are able to do it. I was only pretending not to believe you."

"Oh, you trickster spider," retorted the dwarf, "I know you are only pretending now. I am going to shoot."

"Please do not shoot!" cried Nihancan, but the dwarf answered him, "I must shoot now. When once I have taken up my bow and arrows I must shoot, or I will lose my power."

Then the dwarf lifted his great arrow and aimed and shot. As Nihancan saw the huge tree coming toward him through the air, he began to yell and run first one way and then another. He did not know where to go, for whichever way he went the arrow turned and headed in the same direction. It continued to come nearer and nearer, its point facing directly toward him. Then he threw himself on the soft ground. The tree struck him and forced him deep into the earth, so that only his head was left outside. He struggled to escape, but the arrow wedged him in.

In a short time the dwarf came up to Nihancan, and after scolding him for doubting his strength, he helped him out and gave him some medicine for his bruises. After that Nihancan went on his way, and he never came back to that place again to play tricks on the dwarves.

The children and everyone else applauded loudly, it was a good day.

As evening approached, Nell asked to be taken back inside. It had been a busy day, and she was tired. I had watched her all day. She had eaten very little. I had rejoined the men to share a pipe, and watch the shadows descend on the cliffs opposite the fortress. A chill was in the air. It was evident to all that winter was hiding just over the northern horizon.

Shelly came to the door and called, "Jeff,

come here, quickly."

I got up as quickly as my old bones would let me and hurried inside. Shelly escorted me, saying Nell was asking for me.

I entered the room. My love was lying against a pile of pillows. Her hair had been brushed out, and was a background to her frail body.

I asked, "What is it, Babe? What's wrong?"

She answered, "Oh, nothings wrong, my love. I just wanted you here with me. Jeff, Chris is here. Oh, I know you can't see him, Jeff. He is so proud of you. And, Jeff, you should see him! He is so handsome, I had never thought of him that way. Jeff, he has come to take me to a place to wait for you. I feel so good, I feel like I could run up this mountain again like I used to do when you first brought me here.

"Jeff, don't be sad. Tell all my friends I love them. I have already told Marion and Dave and

Shelly. Tell them everything will be all right, if they just keep going forward.

"Oh, my Darling Jeff! We will be together again before we know it. I love you so much! Thank you for giving me such a wonderful life. I knew if I came with you, it would be that way. I will be waiting for you. Oh, yes, Amigo is here as well. Jeff, Chris is waving for me to come,. I must go now. I...I...I love you...."

Nell closed her eyes, and a calm came over the room. As I sat there, I realized that it was empty now. Someone had gone. It would never be the same again. I climbed up to the bed beside her and lay close to her. I touched her hair, her face. My fingers traced her beautiful lips. This was only a vessel now, that she had treasured. We would take care of it and put it away for her in a proper manner.

I must have lain there for an hour or two. I felt such a loss already, and the days without her had not yet begin to count. I had no thought what I was to do. I had seen death many times in my life, I had always been able to accept it, but this was different.

I slid off the bed and picked up a pad of paper and began to write *Where Have All The Spirits Gone?* When it was finished, I leaned over and kissed her her one more time on the lips. "The last time in this life, Nell," I whispered. I walked out of the room into the living room. There was probably thirty people seated all around the room. Dave walked over and hugged me.

"Jeff, we didn't want you to be alone tonight. Can we stay?"

"Of course you can stay, but we need to get some food started. She wouldn't want us to sit around and starve. And I want to hear some Nell stories."

That evening, Marion and Shelly bathed and dressed Nell in one of her favorite dresses. When they were finished, we all gathered around her and wished her a speedy journey.

I still had not found tears for her, just an incredible ache. We decided not to have her casket open for her funeral, conditions being what they were. We decided the burial would be on the second day after, so that people would be able to come if they wanted. Late the next day the riders started coming in, spreading their bedrolls in the edge of the forest. Next came the wagons circling the perimeters of The Fortress. By evening, the Arapahoe had set a camp near the rest. The vigil began. With almost no words spoken, they came and they sat in a circle near our door, around the deck, some on the deck, quietly, respectfully. All night they sat there. And when morning came, they were still there.

About 9 a.m. James, Mike, Dave Love, Dave Suttle, Randy Wells and Arne carried her casket out to the edge of the deck and sat it on a short platform. Marion and Shelly brought out a host of pictures, all they way back to Nell as a child, then a teenage girl. Then pictures of Nell in her renaissance garb. Then, later pictures here at The Fortress, at the waterfall - clothed of course - and in her beloved greenhouses. On her horse, and with Amigo, and with me, when we were young. Some pictures even I had never seen. They put them around her casket and on the wall, so everyone could see.

Slowly people started to rise and walk around and view the pictures. Some would touch her casket. Tears fell from men and women, and children. It took over an hour for all to pass and pay their respects.

Finally, James arose and said, "We have decided to not have a formal ceremony. Instead, we want to celebrate Nell's life and tell what she has meant to each of us." He went on to tell of his first meeting with Nell, which provoked a bit of laughter. He stopped and said, "Yes, don't be afraid to laugh if something is funny. That is one of the things we will miss most about Nell, her laughter, her joy in life. Nell was happy here with us."

The next was Dave Love, he spoke of meeting Nell sometime before I had met her, how he had loved her for all the time he had known her, and what a hole in his heart she had left. He turned and walked to me and hugged me and sat down with tears in his eyes. The stories went on all morning, thanking Nell for opening her home to them in their darkest hour during the chaos. It was mid-afternoon before the final person had spoken. I stood and walked to Nell's side. I sighed.

"I can't tell all of you what is in my thoughts, or in my memories right now. My heart would not bear it. Instead, I wish each of you to come to me from time to time in the future and tell me your story of Nell, and I will reply with a story of mine. We will only lay her body to rest today. But her spirit, it will be kept alive in all of you. It seems as if she has touched you all. And that is the way I want her to be remembered. I have written a poem to her, in a stumbling way, to try to voice my thoughts. I have asked Marion to read it. I thank you from the bottom of my heart for the respect you have shown her and the kindness you have shown me. Here is Marion."

Marion stood and walked to me turning and hugging me. She spoke, "First, I have loved Nell Bartlett ever since I have known her. She has touched my very soul. When the bad things started to happen in '22, we became even closer. Her strength kept me sane. Her love kept me alive. I will never forget her." She turned and placed her hand softly on Nell's casket, and touched the face of one of the pictures. "Goodbye for a short while, my sweetheart. I will miss you." She turned and faced the people sitting. "Here is Jeff's poem."

Where has all the spirits gone, casting their bodies to earth

Flitting to a distant star, or waiting here for rebirth

Bursting bonds of mortality, like shadowy wings of light

Rising from earthly darkness, to realms that are shining bright

Some say they wait in limbo of purpose not known

I say nay, they have joined friends, and have

reached a happy home

For mortality limits us, and casts a chain to tightly bind

So if logic doth prevail, and I assure you that it must

When that chain be broken, then godly powers will fill our mind

Then past and future, and present, for us to claim

Then our bodies and spirits to us will seem all the same

When soldiers from a battlefield dark, cast down their swords of steel

And meet brothers from battles past, their wounded hearts will heal

When those spirits rise above, trailing tears from ones they love

Be not sad, and lament, for your time soon here is well spent

Be brave old soul, and fear not that day

For then you will be strong again, and your beard will turn from grey

You will climb mountains high, and then you will learn to fly,

It will but require a thought, and just a short blink of an eye

And if it is your Nell that leaves your life

And she was the one only to be your wife

Then let her go, where her pain is not sore

For the day will come, you will walk a shining shore

And laugh again as lovers do

And all you see, will be bright and new

So cry if you must, but let it not last

For soon it will be present, and future, but not past

As the last words were spoken, the men picked up Nell's casket and carried it to the spot where Chris and Amigo lay in their final resting places. It was lowered in to the grave that had been repaired. Several of her friends walked to the side of her grave and tossed in some small gift or memento. John walked to the side of her grave and took an eagle feather, he spoke some words in the Arapahoe tongue, and knelt and dropped it on her coffin. He turned and said, " The evening before last, as I sat outside my door, a White Owl came and flew down and sat on a post near me. It looked at me and flew away toward the east, until I could not see it anymore. I knew that a great being had left the earth." He walked away.

As he did, so did the others, quietly, respectfully. So passed the love of my life, my Nell. She was 59 years old.

April 5, 2040

In the spring after the snow had melted, the country was beginning to come alive. First of all, there were more people alive than we had at first thought. They had fled to remote areas such as we had done. Then, because of the lack of technology and resources, communication went back to early 19th century standards. We didn't even have the telegraph like Civil War era had. But slowly but surely, ham radios sprang up all over the country, and the air came alive. Although the grid was a long way from being alive. We had advanced before Chaos in 2022 with solar and wind power. That was still available. We had been using it from the first, and had installed it as much as possible in all our communities. We were lucky to have lived in a city like Fort Collins, it was a technology center. Although the internet was gone, we could within a few years utilize computers for technical use. Some of the survivors were computer people, and as soon as they were able to take their minds from a survival mode and get them back to their old jobs, things started to happen.

We had scientists all over the country. Well, all of the country that had survived. We started a new Pony Express operation to move documents around where needed. We used the ham radios for the technical people to use to communicate and to organize a rebirth of this country. It wasn't until a year later that we started getting reports from other parts of the world as to the effects of the last twenty years or so.

The first few years of polar melts had caused seas all over the world to rise, and invade some of the largest cities built near the seas.

The United States had long been the leader of

the world in industry, in technology, in transportation, and in energy. And when we fell, it was like a major fumble in the last 10 seconds of the Superbowl. The walls came tumbling down. It would turn out to be a devastating setback for humanity. But it would be a chance to start over, with a new approach to society, for energy, for government, for education. We had been brought to our knees, and now as we struggled to get to our feet. We were like a small child taking his first steps, unsure, careful, but excited. We could learn to walk again.

It seemed our leaders all over were of the same mind - to not make the same mistakes of the past.

I had heard an old fable with a moral many years before. It was about two frogs back in covered wagon days. In that period frogs migrated south for the winter. It was a precarious endeavor, the roads were deeply rutted from the huge wagon wheels. But these little frogs were hopping merrily along chatting about their winter activities, when one of them slipped and fell into a deep rut. Well, he jumped and jumped and clawed and climbed, but alas the rut was to deep. He told his companion, "Kermit, you go on south, before it gets too cold. I will be ok." Kermit said, "But Sam, what will you do?" Sam said, "Aw, don't worry about me. I am kinda comfortable down here in this big ol' rut. I will be fine." So Kermit turned away and continued his journey. After a couple of weeks of travel, he heard a noise behind him. He looked back and as he did, Sam came to a sliding stop beside him, all sweaty and out of breathe. Kermit said "Sam! Sam! What happened? I thought you were all comfortable in your rut?" Sam replied breathlessly, "I was." Kermit asked "What happened?" Sam yelled excitedly, "A WAGON WHEEL CAME ALONG!"

This was the story of America and most of the civilized world. They were comfortable in their rut, and then the wagon wheel of destruction and chaos came along. We don't want to fall back into it again, so this time we take different roads and beware of those ruts.

We still have many challenges ahead of us, we realized the necessity of dialog and debate, so that we can avoid pitfalls on all sides of issues. But although those discussions might be heated, they need to be tempered with reason.

It was easy in the early days for us to live together. We were, for the most part, of like minds. But we were aware as more people came together, that we would have to deal with distension and adversity. It had already occurred somewhat, in some of our trade and some travelers felt they were being subjected to more than their share of hardships. Those were for the most part simple to deal with on a one to one basis.

It was good to meet people from various parts of the country again, and hear stories of their survival and their progress. Many times I wished for my Nell. I had much to do these days, but I was lonely. Having that someone to be with, to share your daily life, to feel the warmth of another body when you go to bed at night, it was something I sorely missed.

Our immediate region, the front range and Wyoming, and some settlements in Nebraska had appointed me an adviser to our High Council. It seemed that because of my foresight in creating a place like The Fortress and helping to administrate it the years following Chaos, they felt I was needed to help ease tensions when discussions became heated. I enjoyed listening to the ideas and theories being debated and voted on, and I felt honored to be recognized as an old greybeard. At heart, I was still just a Texas boy, who had been lucky enough to have a certain old man to point him in a favorable direction. And when I was asked my opinion, I always thought back to what would Chris say or do.

We had formed our governing body, but having the communities each select a man and a woman, basing their choices on those characteristics, that would make a good leader - community service, contributions of talents and time, wisdom and cool headiness. We then sent them to meet with other leaders. No longer would the rich be allowed to buy these positions. Terms of service would be limited to four years. If they went back to their communities after their service and continued to be proper citizens, then after four years, they could be re elected, but no more than two terms would be allowed.

It all seemed to be working for the most part. Other districts liked our model and more and more were adopting it.

On May 1st of 2041, I had the sad duty of going to the memorial service for my good and trusted friend, James Roberts. He had been working with the new Stagecoach Company in Denver, rather, New Denver, just South of old Denver. He had been feeling ill in the after noon, he left work early and went home and went to bed early. Marion said he never woke up. His big caring, responsible heart just quit beating. I had gone to Denver by stage coach and retrieved his body and Marion. Marion and I talked on the long overnight ride back to Rustic. Now it was time to say goodbye to my friend for the last time. I spoke of our friendship, of his devotion to others, of how he would be the last to quit his responsibility, or to sit and rest or eat a meal. I laughed and mentioned his love of good Colorado Bud, and how he was the master of breeding and growing the finest of hybrids. He also was the one that started our hemp fields, and promoting the various industries we were starting to develop from it. He was a powerhouse that would be missed. His remembrance was attended by a huge crowd of friends. After everyone had left, Marion and I sat on the small deck behind the community center overlooking the Poudre River. We sat for a long time. I held her hand. I knew what she was feeling. At 61, she had lost the only companion she had ever been with. I knew in her mind, she was wondering where to go, what direction to follow. I knew as the days went on that her life would resume, but it would be difficult starting.

"Marion, I have room at The Fortress. I would like for you to come and stay with me. I could use your help these days. I think Nell would have liked to see you there."

"Thanks, Jeff, I might just do that. I always loved it up there. Since James and I never had any family, I really don't have a place to go. We gave up our place there on the mountain, Chase McCullom and his new bride needed a place of their own, and we were spending so much time here at Rustic and in New Denver, I really don't have another place. Yes, there are so many good memories there. Nell and I were girls in that greenhouse there. Yes, I will. Thank you."

The next morning early I had a carriage brought around and we were driven to The Fortress, arriving late afternoon, just before sundown. Brian and Danny and Dave Love were waiting for us, each hugging Marion and expressing their condolences. We sat on the deck and had a light dinner and talked till the evening chill drove us inside. Marion excused herself and went to her room exhausted from the day.

I had taken to writing in the evenings. Arne

and one of his young men had gotten me a computer working and repaired an ancient printer. I sat about remembering all those things from our lost world, and trying to document them in the true light they reflected, be it bad or good. Too soon things are forgotten, then remembered in a different way than they really were. I didn't want history to be forgotten and then remembered falsely.

In our past people had taken history, our Constitution, even the Bible, for those that followed it, and interpreted them for their own benefit. I knew it could happen again, and probably would. So many of us that had lived before Chaos were now growing old. So many of the young only had tales to go by. That wasn't enough. The history of the twenty or so years before Chaos would be lost to mankind, for it never got written and was lost before it could be judged. That was dangerous. I felt someone should record it. I would try to find others to help before we were gone as well.

At 73, I was still healthy and strong. My mind

was clear, and I was saddled with the responsibility of helping our new world progress. I searched for others as old as myself or older who remembered what life in our past had been. Some were just old and had become sedate, some didn't care to remember. One day, a message was given me about a Monastery of Buddhist monks living high in the mountains above Telluride, Colorado. I asked Marion to help me prepare for the journey. It would take several days to reach them, by stage coach and carriage.

Leaving out of Denver by stage, we climbed up through the canyons and over Kenosha Pass, changing teams quite often in those first hundred miles or so. As we headed out across the broad expanses of South Park, past the old towns of Jefferson and Fairplay, huge herds of elk grazed in the meadows, and from time to time, herds of buffalo. It was late June. Anciently, the Ute had said that the buffalo came to South Park in June. It must look much as it did in the mid 1800's. The old Highway 285, was still in fair condition. We rolled, making probably much better time then did the stages of the early west. Down through Trout Creek Pass, spending one night in Johnsons Village. Then on to Poncha Pass for another night. The old town of Salida lay down the road a few miles to the east. I had been there several times in the early years. It sat on the banks of the Arkansas River. It had been an artist town, and very pleasant to visit, lying in a valley between the Mosquito Range, The Collegiates, and the Sangre de Cristos Mountains. The waitress in the dining room at the stage stop in Poncha Springs said people were starting to come back and rebuild the town. This valley had been known for it's climate and it's ability to produce food in the early part of the 20th century. It was starting to do it again.

The next day we spent crossing Monarch Pass, although the high mountain climate and scenery was exhilarating, I found it a bit breathtaking, literally. I got just a bit winded over the pass, but other than a slight headache, all was well. Days went by as we traveled through the old town of Gunnison and then past Blue Mesa Reservoir. I had been by it in the past by auto. I was amazed it seemed as if we traveled by it for ever, then we crossed the dam and followed the steep canyon known as the Black Canon of the Gunnison. It was a sight that made me wish I had the talent of a painter I was like a small boy at Disneyland, back years ago. Each turn, a new sight to see.

At the old town of Montrose we traveled south to Ridgeway, then started to climb again. it was late the next day when my carriage brought me to the Monastery, a place of simple but exquisite beauty. I was greeted by a young Asian man dressed in saffron robes. He took me down a long hallway and placed me in a comfortable room in a easy chair, and said, in very good English, "Relax, sir, you will be joined shortly."

I did as he said. I was served with a cup of tea, and some simple but delicious cakes.

As I was sipping the last of my tea, a door opened and four men entered and, bowing slightly, seated themselves at the table before me. Each introduced himself to me. The leader, spoke last.

"Jeff Bartlett, it is an honor to meet you. We have heard of your community. We have also heard of your philosophy, and we admire it. What can we do to be of service to you?"

I told him of my search for people that had lived in the early part of our century and still had the memories of how life was. How I wanted to document their stories for future generations, of my difficulties in finding the kinds of people I needed.

He answered, "An admirable task, for if one is not a student of the mistakes and achievements of the past, how will it be possible to both avoid and grasp those ideas in the future?"

We talked for several hours. I felt at ease with these men, almost comforted just being in their presence. I was told that they had a surprise for me on the morrow. I was given quarters for the evening. A simple room with simple furnishings, but comfortable. I was asleep quickly.

I awoke to the sound of chanting, beautiful sounds that I had never heard before. I dressed and went outside. I walked down a hallway to a beautiful garden. There, at the end of the garden on a raised platform, sat about 15 or so robed figures. The sounds were coming from them. I moved back out of the garden into the hallway and sat on a bench. I listened, mesmerized by what I heard. The sounds of their chants seemed to energize me as well as calm me.

Too soon they ended. I was directed into a room with a long table where I was seated with the monks. Food was brought in and consumed. Then the leader came and beckoned for me to follow him. We passed through the garden, and into another garden. In it were seated about six men and maybe 8 women.

"Jeff Bartlett, I will leave you to get acquainted. I believe the Christian Bible has a verse that says, 'Ask and it shall be given unto you'. Well, you have asked."

I turned to face the men and women seated about the room. A lady stood. She was tall and slender, her snow white hair braided into a long braid that hung down her back to her waist. She wore an almost floor length simple dress that fit her very tastefully.

She smiled and said, "Good morning Mr. Bartlett. We have been anxiously waiting you."

"But, how, did you know I was coming?" I stammered. I was very much surprised at seeing these people in this place.

"Some of your letters, your writings, your questions have reached us."

I spent the entire morning meeting these people. One, a famous writer of the late twentieth century. Another, a Doctor. An Artist, A U.S. Senator from Utah, and a Congressman from Colorado. Others from the fields of education and public service. One of the men was a man of Vietnamese descent. As he spoke, I realized something familiar about him, and when he told his story about his escape from Vietnam and coming to Houston to study, suddenly I knew him.

I interrupted him, apologizing for doing so, asking him, "Do you remember a young man taking GED classes with you, and sometimes gave you rides?"

He jumped from his chair throwing his arms about me, "My Brother! It was you, Mister Jeff! I sensed something about you. Oh, my friend! So many times have I thought about you and your welfare. I am so glad to see you once more!"

His name was Dr. Du Hua. He had become a famous and respected Pharmacist and researcher, in the field of medicines before the Chaos.

I was amazed and energized. Here were some of the best brains from our lost world. And better than that, they, too, had realized the errors of the past. I spent days talking, making notes. The priests loaned us two young ones of their groups to help us document our efforts. At one point I realized I had been gone for over a week. It was with deep sorrow that I realized that I must take my leave.

Our last evening was spent rehashing the events of the extreme chaos of 2022 and 2023. Each had realized that they were in danger and had traveled by plane and car, anyway they were able to make it to this Shangri La, here in the Rockies. They had helped the priests to defend it in the early days, and had added their own talents to the high capabilities of the priests to aid in their survival. Now, as they had grown old, they found happiness living in their small group and spending their last days in a community of like minds. I envied them. I knew I would be happy to stay here indefinitely. But I also felt the call to get back to my own communities and tell them of the things I had learned, of the ideas that had been proposed.

So as our evening grew to a close. Catherine Noble, the lady I had described earlier, came forward. She handed me a large briefcase of almost suitcase size.

"Jeff, we want you too take this with you. See that it is applied and shared with as many as would want to share it. It is copies of our ideas and observations over the years, warnings of pitfalls that can harm our new and fragile small world. It also contains copies of all our biographies, and accomplishments of the past. We have included ideas for technology that can be developed fairly quickly, and with low impact. New ideas that may be enlarged upon by some of your smart people that you seem to have surrounded yourself with. Jeff, this may be your most revered legacy that will be remembered in the history of our world, that you did know how to find these people that were doers, and held the high ideals that you seem to hold dear.

"Mr. Bartlett, it has been a pleasure to have spent this time with you. And you give us hope that a new, exciting world can be built again. Go, with our blessings and hopes to a new future."

"Catherine, how can I ever thank you. All of you. You have given me hope. I will always treasure this last week. I will go and tell our communities about you. Maybe we can have other representatives come and visit. Perhaps our educators, our community leaders. We all need to be inspired as you have inspired me, if that would acceptable."

"That would be very acceptable. It would give our lives purpose. We love that, it give us a chance to be a part of this new beginning."

I spent the last hours with Du Hua. I told him of my Nell and how she had suffered. I told him how we so needed medicine and surgeons and doctors. He agreed and said he would make it one of his top priorities and I would be hearing from him soon.

After saying my goodbyes individually, I retired to my small quarters. Sleep came with great difficulty that night, if it came at all. Morning came with a soft knock at my door. I dressed quickly and found my carriage waiting outside the gate. I turned for one last look back at a place I had never knew existed a short time back. Yet, it had given me new purpose in life. I stepped aboard, and in a short time was boarding my stagecoach for the ride home. The mountains were beautiful, but I saw little of them. I wrote notes and plans where the road was smooth enough, and spent my time in meditation on the chores ahead. I did talk in some length with my fellow passengers, discussing ideas as we traveled, and gleaned some valuable input.

Days later as the coach arrived at Rustic – now renamed Phoenix by it's community. I was thrilled to see Marion waiting for my arrival. I stepped down and received an affectionate hug, accompanied by a whispered, "I missed you."

We took our quarters at 'Phoenix' for that

evening. It would take some time before I would get used to calling it by that name.

Early that evening we gathered in the community center. My purpose was to brief the leaders on the events of the last weeks. It turned out to be that more than the leaders who wanted to be briefed. I waited until about seven-ish, and all the chores were done. A crowd of people had taken all the seats and crowded around the wall, waiting patiently for news from that outside world that so many never got to experience anymore. I stood to speak.

"My friends and neighbors, you have no idea how good it feels to be once again in your company. I had a much enjoyable trip, and a very profitable trip for us all. But there truly is no place like home. Upon leaving Rustic....I mean Phoenix, excuse me. Old habits die hard." A light chuckle passed through the room.

"I traveled to New Denver, then up over Kenosha Pass to South Park. I was much impressed with the amount of native animals that have increased in the mountain regions. I could but wonder how it must have looked to our forefathers in the 1800's. I am proud to report that there are small groups of people here and there, some are struggling. But there is a unity among all of us that, because of the history of the early part of this century, we might not have suspected. We pray that continues. My journey was good, but the best part was when I arrived at my destination."

I recounted my introduction to the "sages" and our talks and planning. As I named some of the people I had met, there were murmurs of recognition. I told the story of meeting an old friend, now famous in the field of medicine. As I ended my narrative, questions came from every part of the room, Another hour was spent in answering. Indeed, at the end of the evening, those in attendance seemed to be as excited as I was. When I announced that different ones of our community would have opportunities to travel to Telluride and attend seminars in their career fields, a great round of applause went up.

Shortly after retiring to my cabin, I received a knock at my door. I answer, "Enter!" and the door opened. It was Marion.

"Jeff, can I visit a moment?"

"Of course, Marion, come in." I had already undressed and had crawled into bed. Marion simply dropped her robe. She was dressed only in a night shirt. She slipped under the covers with me, and snuggled up to my shoulder. She looked up at me.

"Is this alright? I am so damned lonely."

I smiled at her. "Dearest Marion, it is much more than alright. It is much desired. For friends like us to be able to be close and be a comfort to each other at this point in life, and after losing our life partners, is, well, we are very lucky. And I have loved you for years. However, if you are looking for a romantic partner, you just might have come to the wrong place."

"Jeff, you dunce! I am not interested in that at all anymore!"

We lay in each others arms for a while. I could almost see Nell and James smiling down on us, and nodding their approval. They would understand. Two lost souls, trapped in mortality, finding solace in each others arms while they waited to be with their lovers.

We drifted into a deep slumber, refusing to let go of each other, barely changing positions all night. Waking in the morning, a bit embarrassed at the newness, but still feeling like lovers on their honeymoon. It was so good to hold someone close again.

We dressed and chatted happily at each other. I was anxious to get back to The Fortress. So much to do.

As we walked out the door, we met face to face with Dave Suttle.

He smiled and said, "You two took, like, forever to arrive at this point. I kept waiting. Wondering what was taking you so long. I and some of your friends had considered kidnapping the two of you and locking you in a room together until you got the idea that everyone knew you should have. Congratulations, you two. You will be very happy together."

I turned to Marion, saying, "Isn't it wonderful that all these people know what's best for us?"

She raised up and kissed me full on the lips, saying, "Yes!"

After breakfast, a meeting was convened. I opened the suitcase/briefcase I had been presented with. The next four hours we spent seperating different portions to different committees. Brian and Danny became quite excited over some of the material they were given. When I asked why, they replied that they had been working on these ideas for years. Now they would be able complete their projects. They wouldn't tell me what as yet, they said they wanted it to be a surprise. The day before, on way home, I had noticed some giant wheels being built in the river, along with some large structures resembling towers. I was really curious about them.

I saw Arne coming up the trail from the river. I waited. When he reached me, I had to ask.

"Arne, what is with this building on the river?"

He smiled, "Thought you would never ask, Jeff. Remember in your history books, how both Washington and Jefferson had this dream of linking the country by using the rivers?"

"Yes, I remember it very well."

"Well, this an experiment. If it works it can be utilized in rivers all over the country, no, all over the world. Some rivers, like the Poudre, aren't really navigate-able by boat. Yet they travel distances sometimes."

"You are right. How does it work?"

"Well, some of us got the idea from the ski lifts. Bbut instead of powering them from gas or electric motors, we are using water wheels. We also have rigged zip lines for getting people down the canyon in a hurry. So far, so good. We are still scrounging cable, but if this gets big, we will have to utilize another method."

"Wow. Great idea, Arnie, go for it. Keep me posted."

"Will do, Jeff, will do!"

Next morning we left our friends at new Phoenix and made the trip back to The Fortress. It was good to be home. We thanked our carriage driver and he and his companion turned away to return to their base. Travel in our area had become more organized this past year. We were getting more and more traffic through our towns. Max had mentioned that people were starting to open some resorts up the mountains above old Centennial, Wyoming this past summer to get away from the heat.

It was starting to concern me that no one seemed interested in developing new technology. It seemed that people were happy living in this redefined nineteenth century world. When I would mention it, the usual answer would be.

"Well, that is what got us into this mess wasn't it?"

Well, yes, it was. But still there is a necessity that humanity moves forward. True, it should move forward cautiously, but it still should move forward.

As winter came on in this year of '41, I thought a lot about our medical levels. I had sent one of our nurses to Telluride a month ago. She had returned, stating the doctors there wanted to start training young doctors for surgery using cadavers again. I had told her to select some students she thought would be best and send them out. My thoughts went to Nell. Had we been more prepared, maybe, just maybe.....

Winter dragged on. It seemed like forever. I was starting to have some motor function issues, especially in cold weather. It was a bit harder to stand up on these cold days, but I was still a lucky man health wise.

One cold winter evening, as Marion and I were holed up in our bedroom reading, she asked, "Jeff, all the years I have known you, I have never heard you speak of your family. Is it ok if I ask you about them?"

I looked up from my book, and thought for a moment. I didn't think of that part of my life anymore!

"No, Marion, it is fine. There is not much to tell, sometime in 1979 or 80, my parents had a bad auto accident. They were both killed. I had a baby brother, he was put in a foster home, or rather foster homes. I was about twelve, and he about two. I went to two or three different homes over the course of a couple of years. The last family wanted to adopt me, but they wouldn't let me keep my name. I was about 15 then. I ran away. I lived by hook or crook, on the streets in Austin mostly. It was several years later that the old man found me and straightened my young ass out."

"What happened to your baby brother?"

"I am not really sure. I tried to find him. I found the family that had fostered him. They said a woman who said she was his aunt took him. I know my mother had a sister, her name was Jean. I tried to find her, but the last name I remembered didn't turn up anything. After all this, I am not sure anymore. I don't know where he is."

"That's too bad. So many people have died. All my family were east coast people, I'm sure they are all gone. So sad."

"Marion, we don't want civilization to ever go that route again. We simply must educate, educate, educate. And what worries me , is we still don't know the conditions in Europe, or

Asia. I always fear an invasion. We simply don't know."

At times like these, I felt like one of our Native Americans in 1450, wondering if there was anything on the other side of the big waters.

Our world in 2022, was a global society, in almost every way. Every facet of our lives depended on something maybe 10,000 miles away. Electronics, especially in communications, was off the chart in development. We all took it for granted. A good part of everything bought and sold was done on the internet, even ordering food, by restaurant, and by store. The stores were linked by computer to the warehouses, warehouse to meat and produce houses, to trucking companies. It was really lucky to keep two weeks of food on hand in almost any city in America. It didn't take much, to set the world in Chaos. Within days of the shutdown, the stores were, for the most part, empty. Within a week, nothing edible remained. Think for a moment. You are living in downtown, or even suburbs, of Houston, Dallas, Vegas, anywhere. Suddenly, an event occurs, and technology shuts down. You look in your refrigerator, and milk, cheese, meat, is low. *Hmmm*, you think, *maybe I had better run to the store.* You holler out, *Hey Honey, I am going to the store.*

You go jump in your 2019 Kia and run down to Kroger's. you think, *Gee, sure is crowded*. As you go inside, you hear people shouting at each other at the meat counter. *Wonder what that's about?* You hurry on to the milk counter. It's empty. You ask one of the clerks, "Do you have any more milk in the back?"

"No, sir. We are out today."

You pick up part of the items you came for, and decide to pass on the rest. You wait in line with a bunch of angry people. You study them with a bit of amazement. You pay for your purchases. On the way out of the parking lot you noticed you fuel gauge is only on half, but every fuel stop you see is just far to crowded to attempt. So you drive back home and tell your wife or husband about your experiences of the last hour. They shrug and pass it off as coincidence.

That evening you turn on the 6 o'clock news and a local news anchor is all excited about arrest being made for assaults in food stores and fuel stops all over the town, indeed all over the country.

Two days later, your food stores are completely gone. Your Kia is out of fuel, and there is no heat or A/C in your house. Your toilet won't flush. There is no water, or power, your flashlights have run out of batteries, and there is no phone service, no one to call upon for help. Worse of all, those nice neighbors across the street and next door have suddenly become cruel and hateful people. So, what do you do? A good many people will try to hole up in their homes. Bad decision. Now they are stuck, with nothing. And remember, things are not getting any better outside. Bands of takers will roam the streets, trying to get necessities or whatever by force. This isn't 'A kinder gentler society' . When people are scared and hungry, they will mostly revert to animalistic behavior. Ask any soldier who has ever been on a battlefield in a fallen country. He will tell you.

All pets, cats, dogs, horses, whatever will be consumed first. Within the first month, cannibalism will break out. Maybe not murder, but the weak and infirm will die first. They will be consumed. Then the victims of accidents, then will come the hunted.

There were some then that were seeking balance in the world, seers that knew the possibilities of what could happen. They were ignored, put aside as doomsayers.

But this was 2042, twenty years had gone by, progress had been made. A thing to think about, it would have been an impossible task if more of the population had survived. A sad fact, but a true one. I sometimes think that is the way nature intended it, for the earth to only support a population that was self sustaining!

As I said before, education, education, education, people must see what errors in life can bring you too! Learn from history, not ignore it!

Idaho

Damien sat looking over the back of the three mules hooked ahead of him. The rail trailers rolled easily on the level plains of northern Wyoming, they were half way across. The trip had made good progress. On some of the uphills they would have to hitch other teams to outriggers on the wagons so that the horses could walk on the outside of the rails on each side, sometimes two teams on each side on the longer grades. But it was all working out. They had come to a couple of trestles. When the did, they unhooked the teams and led them around the trestle to the other side, then hooked ropes and pulled the wagons across. Water was a bit of a problem, but they managed to keep enough, and there was forage for the animals, even the cows. All twenty-five of them when they started, now there was 28. Three new calves delayed them some. Sometimes the calves were carried and sometimes they walked. Oh, yeah, a new baby. Named Moses, 'cause he was born on an exodus. Damien looked up ahead. A rider was coming to meet them. It was

Russ, he had been scouting ahead. He approached, and turned his horse to walk alongside.

"Hey, Dad, about three miles up ahead we have a nice big creek with a really good place to camp, maybe fish some. I saw several brookies. I vote we spend a day there. We will have to tow the wagons across anyway. Give everyone a bit of a rest."

Damien frowned. He hated delaying their progress, but yelled back, "Ok, lead on McDuff!"

Russ flashed a smile back at his father, "Great! I will ride back and tell the others."

Shortly Damien heard cheering. *I guess it was a well favored decision, he thought.* About an hour later they topped a small rise and could see a line of trees ahead of them lining a stream. Damien applied just a bit of brake so the trailer wouldn't push the mules.

It was a great camping spot. Several of the couples, after setting up camp, went off in different directions to have a bit of privacy for bathing. Soon fires were going and the smell of food being prepared drifted. Hunters had shot a couple of deer and some pronghorn for dinner.

After all were fed, someone pulled out their guitar and was singing, *'Home, home on the range'....* She reworded it somewhat, to reflect the immediate travels. Everyone was having a good laugh. Laughing was good. Yeah, maybe an extra day would be good.

When Damien awoke the next morning, the sun was already up. But a heavy fog hung over the stream. Damien looked up. On a small knoll about 50 yards above him stood ten riders, shrouded by the fog, as it partially hid then revealed them. They appeared to be Native American, but were dressed in western denim. They sat motionless on their horses, as if waiting.

Damien arose and dressed, and went out of

his tent. He walked toward the riders, hoping for the best. As he reached them, one of the riders stepped down. He turned and walked toward him.

"Hi, I am Damien Bradley."

"Hello, I am Michael Grey Fox. Where you folks headed?"

"We are moving down to a colony we have heard about near the City of Fort Collins, Colorado."

"Yes, Jeff Bartlett's community. I know it well. In fact, part of our tribe is living near there."

Damien's legs almost buckled, he felt queasy and giddy. He sat down on a large boulder.

"Did you say Jeff Bartlett? How old a man is he? What does he look like?"

"Oh, 'bout your size, little older though. Maybe in his mid seventies, why?"

Damien could hardly speak, "He may be my older brother!" he stammered.

"Humph, maybe. There is a resemblance. You have several weeks of travel, we will be there before you. Do wish me to tell him?"

"No, No. Just in case it doesn't work out. I had rather meet him myself, people change over the years."

"Not Jeff. He never changes! He is a good man."

"Nevertheless."

"I understand. But to shorten the time, I will tell him that a wagon train of immigrants is coming in, and I think he should go meet them."

"Very well. I will agree with that. Come, get off your horses and come have some coffee and breakfast."

As they walked back talking, the camp had come to life. Clusters of people were standing and watching. As the men came into camp some of the younger boys of the camp took their horses and tied them on a picket. The men sat around the table that had been put up for serving purposes. Damien introduced Michael and Russ. He told Russ about what Michael had told him about Jeff Bartlett. Russ' only remark was, "Hot Damn!"

After breakfast, the Arapahoe men helped them snake their wagons across the trestle and soon after bid their goodbyes, with a promise to meet again in a few weeks. They soon afterward disappeared into the high plains of Wyoming to the southwest.

For the next weeks the days were uneventful, if not a bit boring. They traveled by day, slept under the beautiful Wyoming skies at night, filled with trillions of stars. They watched planets race across the sky at night, as probably did ancient man. They were learning to be in awe of life again. They sat out at night and talked to the children about how life had once been. They told them how man had started to take his life for granted, and the life of this planet they lived on. They started to talk about the circle of life, called the four seasons, and how man was dependent on them. The schooling took on a different attitude than children experienced before the disaster had occurred.

It was the end of June. Damien knew they were getting close to their destination. He was a impatient wreck, the thought that this Jeff Bartlett might be his brother haunted his ever waking moment. He dared not hope so strongly, less he might come to a horrible disappointment. Nevertheless, he couldn't help it.

Finally on July 1st they could see the north end of the front range of the Colorado Rockies. His wait was almost over, soon he would know.

They rolled up to the downtown area of old Fort Collins on the morning of July 3rd. A fairly large group of people awaited them with dozens of empty wagons. It was a humbling feelings to see so many helping hands welcoming them to their new home. Damiens' eyes searched the crowd for a face that he might know, but it was a futile gesture in the midst of so much activity. He recognized a couple of the young Arapahoe men that had met them on the way in, but no one with them appeared to be right. In truth, he knew not what or who to expect. Finally, the young Arapahoe with another man approached.

"Mr. Bradley, would you come with us? Mr. Bartlett is waiting in his carriage for you."

∞

The spring of '42 was shaping to be a good year for all, it gave me hope that our society was on a good track, and ready to grow. Our mentors in Telluride had been active in working with our smartest students. We just recently had developed a new battery technique. It was a fixed system, good only for storing energy for homes or businesses, but it was a huge breakthrough, as all the batteries from before Chaos had been recycled so many times their lives were very short. The new technique was a much longer lasting one and I was sure as the experts worked with it, it would be even better. Now, though, we wanted to develop portable batteries for transportation. That was more difficult, but we would succeed. Marion and I were spending much of our time these days at New Phoenix. We enjoyed the social life there. We had turned a little resort community into a thriving city. I say we, meaning the community in general. And it was a self sustaining city, each home and each business, was a stand alone entity.

About the third week of June, Michael Grey

Fox and some of his companions had ridden into The Fortress and informed me of a band of immigrants that were approaching from Washington State. He said they had visited with them, and was quite impressed with the quality of the people in that community. He said he estimated their arrival about the first of July, and he felt that I should meet them and welcome them. The fact that Michael was that impressed with them was reason enough for me to make that happen. I told him I would be there and thanked him for letting me know. So the next week Marion and I took a carriage down to New Phoenix. On the afternoon of July 2nd, a message came that the immigrants would be in Fort Collins some time on the 3rd. On the morning of the 3rd, Marion and I took the new zip-line down to the mouth of the canyon. It only took a little over a half hour to make the trip. It had been an impressive endeavor, though it had many mistakes and problems in the early days, and a few accidents, but was worth the effort.

A carriage was waiting at the foot of the

canyon, and little while later we were waiting at the railroad crossing at old Mulberry Street. Shortly that afternoon, we saw the big mule pulled wagons coming in. I was impressed. I turned to Dave Suttle and said, "David, that is a really good idea. I wished I had thought of it."

David laughed, "Yeah, maybe that guy is your brother or something."

I looked at David. What a strange thing to say.

As the wagons approached, the crowd gathered close to the tracks. We had brought many wagons so the people and their goods could be moved to a suitable site that we had prepared just west of the old town of La Porte below Horsetooth Reservoir.

Marion and I sat in the carriage, waiting for the bustle to subside. In a few minutes, David and Michael approached leading a man in his mid-sixties, I assumed that he must be the leader of the group, so I stepped down from the carriage. The gentleman approached me, and something about him seemed almost unsettling.

He stood in front of me and asked, "Are you Jeff Bartlett?"

"I am, Sir. And who might you be?"

"Jeff, my name is Damien Bradley. I think I am your younger brother."

I looked at him. My senses reeled, and I fell back against the carriage. David grabbed me to steady me. I could find no words for what seemed like minutes on end.

Finally, I managed, "How can that be? How did you find me, are you all alone? How do you know for sure?"

Damien replied, "If you lost your parents in an auto accident about 1980 in Spokane, and was separated from your brother, you were about 12 and I was two, then we know for sure."

I could scarce believe what I was hearing! Yet it was true, I knew it. I reached for my brother, throwing my arms around his neck. Tears were flowing. *Oh my God, a miracle, at seventy-four!* I have a brother!

"Damien, how did you know I was here?" I couldn't turn loose of him even for a moment, but finally I released him and stepped back. As I looked around, every one of my friends were busy wiping eyes or blowing noses. Marion's face was wet with tears.

I looked at David, "You knew!"

"Not for sure, Jeff. Michael thought so, and we wanted to wait and see. So very happy for you, and Damien. You are both fine men and it was only right that you find each other."

It was about that time that I noticed others gathering around. Damien had recovered and started introductions. "Jeff, this Sandy, my wife.

This is my son Russ and his wife Misty, and this is little Todd, my grandson. And this is my daughter Cissy and her husband Brad." I went to each one and hugged them. When I got to little Todd, I broke down in tears again. I turned to Damien.

"It would be rewarding enough to get a brother, but to get a whole family, it almost to much for the emotions to handle. But enough for now, all of you have had a long journey, we must get you settled.

"We have coaches and wagons to move everyone to a temporary site until we can get you permanently settled. David, give our carriage to someone. Marion and I are going to take one of the big coaches with the family and go to the hotel at Ted's Place for tonight and get some food and some rest. And visit, visit, visit!"

We all crowded into the big coach and found comfortable positions and head back to Ted's Place to the hotel we had built for travelers coming through and staying for a day or so.

Damien broke the silence.

"Jeff, I was sitting in my wagon as we arrived. I searched the crowd for you, I have not rested, since I found out my brother might be alive and near to me. As I watched Michael and David approached me, he introduced me to David, and told me to come with them. I hardly remember the 30 or 40 yard walk to your carriage, and when my gaze finally fell on you, my heart fairly jumped out of my chest. You look like father would have looked, had he lived to be your age. I knew then, but I wanted to be sure."

I answered, "I have wondered all these years where you might be, or if you might be, especially after Chaos. So many people died. I tried to find you when I was in my late teens and early twenties. I knew someone had adopted you, probably our mother's sister, but the name I knew her by seemed not to exist. Finally, I gave up, and life was not really good to me back then. I was surviving by hook or crook, with a lot of crook. I got on the wrong side of the law a few times. God knows what might have happened to me, had I not ran into an old man by the name of Chris Bowen who straightened me out and became my friend and mentor for years."

"Jeff, I was lucky. Yes it was my Aunt Jean who who adopted me. she passed in 2022, shortly before the disaster. She was good to me and gave me a good upbringing and a good life. She tried many times to find you, but her resources were limited. After you had run away from your foster home, and went to Austin, it was like looking for a needle in a haystack.

"One more thing, do you have any children?"

"No, my first wife, Nell, and I never had children. And Marion and I, after Nell passed away, well, we were just too old for that sort of thing. But if it is ok with you, I am just going to consider yours mine, and spoil them all to death."

"Of course, Brother. I wouldn't have it any other way," Damien laughed.

Our laughter and conversation was scarcely interrupted by our arrival at the hotel. Rooms were assigned, and people were bathed and dressed in clean clothing and gathered once again for our first family dinner. Not only our family, but also my family of close friends. The McCulloms', with their children and grand children, David and David, and Arne, and Charles's widow and children. Everyone that could be there was there.

After dinner, I stood and tapped on a glass, and asked if I might say a few words.

"Friends, family. I want to try to express what is in my heart tonight. These here on my right are my dear brother and his family that have appeared out of the northwest, like a spring thunderstorm, bringing a life giving refreshment to the green grass of an old mans heart. I wish you to welcome them into your hearts and lives as I will over the coming days. They bring talents and energies that are going to help push our lives forward again. They, like so many that have joined us, are like a transfusion of energy and talents and knowledge that would take us countless years to discover by ourselves. This we know. We are not a single cell that stands alone, for it cannot grow past it's own, but we are a collection of cells that join together to create a new being, one that will join with another being, to create a community. Otherwise, when that cell reached it's maturity and passed, there would be no more.

"Damien, Sandy, older and younger children. I like to introduce those that have been my family for the past years. Here is Marion. She was the wife of one of my best friends James Roberts. James passed away not too long after my Nell passed. Our lives were so empty after that, and having known each other for some many years, it was only fitting that our lives would drift together. This is my friend Dave Love. We have known each other for years, and long ago became brothers, not of blood, but of caring for each other. Next, the McCulloms'. Again, family because of ties, too deep to be anything else. Mike has been my right hand for so long, I would feel like an amputee were he not there. Then,

Dave Suttle. Dave is the son I never had. He is one of the reasons we are still here and still moving forward. This bunch over here is Charles Well's family. Charlie, sadly is no longer with us. We miss his fine spirit and wisdom daily, but he left us a fine family as his legacy. Now I am going to shut up and sit down. The next few days will be busy, but tomorrow is the Fourth of July, and we are all going to new Phoenix for the celebration."

The next morning, we boarded the river lift, Marion and I and Damien's family. It took us up river in about an hour and a half, faster than a coach, but oh, what a splendid view! About twelve feet above the Poudre river, up the canyon we went, looking upward at the mountainside and the cliffs. Here and there, bighorn sheep looked down at us. An occasional eagle swished by, looking for a shallow fish. In the upper valleys, elk and buffalo grazed.

When we reached the landing at New Phoenix our car was derailed to a side rail for us to unload. As soon as we did the attendant put it back on the main line and down the river it went again. As we walked up from the river to the community center, I put my arm around my brother's shoulders and whispered, "Damien, I still remember the awe of holding you on my lap as a baby, and knowing you were my brother. The years have been cruel, but let's not waste a day. I would like to prepare you and Sandy a house near to Marion and myself, so we can visit whenever we wish. I don't want to ever be far from you again."

"Jeff, that would be wonderful! I would love that, and whatever assistance I can be, count on me."

"I would like to make my house at the Fortress available to Russ and Misty, and Cissy and Brad. It needs young people again. Nell and I had our finest years there. It is a good place for young people."

We arrived at New Phoenix as the Fourth of July celebration reached full swing. We walked and talked to neighbors. I introduced our family around. I was still in a bit of a daze, and had to keep pinching my self to assure that I wasn't dreaming. Finally Damien and myself sat our weary bones down in a shade, and proceeded to east an ice cream dish that had been prepared. Mine was Peach and Damien chose Strawberry. As we ate, Damien looked up at the big greenhouses above us.

"Jeff, it is remarkable what you have done here. You people have worked together and created a very good, and from all observances, a happy life here. I know assuredly that Sandy and Misty are going to be up there as soon as they are invited."

"Good thought. As soon as everyone has eaten we will go up and show you around."

By early afternoon everyone had eaten and conversed. So I gathered my new family about me and we walked the short climb up the side of the hill to the pathway between two of the large greenhouses. We climbed the stairway to the back side and entered the west greenhouse. As soon as we stepped inside, my thoughts went to Nell, and all her efforts in making these giant entities come to life. Inside, the first sight was three peach trees laden with fruit. I picked a nice one and pulled it open. This tree was a peach known as a freestone. You could pull it apart with your fingers and remove the seed. I handed the peach to little Todd. He took it and cautiously took a bite, and immediately yelled,

"Mom, this good!"

To which everyone had a good laugh. As we walked the terraces out from the wall, we came to the hanging tomato plants. Their roots growing in a slow moving water trough. They, too, were loaded with fruit.

Misty laughed, "Oh MY Gawd! I could spend the rest of my life in here! Russ, bring me a bed, I will live here."

I smiled, "Misty hon, I hate to disappoint you, but you can't do that." Her smile started to melt,

I hurriedly added, "You are going to have your own greenhouse. I have spoken to Damien, and I want you and Russ and Cissy and Brad to take my house at The Fortress. You will love it there. There is room for both families, and it has two large greenhouses, just waiting for you. It is a beautiful place, but it cries for young people."

Her smile lit up and tears came to her eyes.

"Oh, Uncle Jeff! Thank you! I wondered how long it would be before I was able to have a home again! Thank you so much," as she came and put both arms around my neck and hugged me.

"We will get your community in order in the next couple of days, and get them settled in, get all your goods moved up. I will send some wagons down and have you guys' stuff moved up to The Fortress, and then Marion and I will take you over to your new home. Damien, Sandy, I would love for you to go with us.

"Russ, you and Brad go down tomorrow and get your goods separated out. Damien, on second thought, if you will, we will go as well and have yours brought up. We need to get your livestock located where they are handy to you as well."

After our evening meal of elk burgers and sausages roasted over an open fire, we settled in for the evenings entertainment. Tonight was two different bands, affording dancing for everyone. I danced with my favorite girl, then with Sandy, and finally with Misty and Cissy. It was refreshing to hold a young body in my arms again. It had been sometime now. I was reminded of the energy that is born of youth. I thought that it was well that it was designed as such. They had the responsibility of powering those acts to keep humanity moving, to push progress ahead of them, to bear children, and to keep up with those children until they reached responsible age. So that vibrancy that I felt in those young bodies was placed there for definite purpose.

As the band played their last number, I was told that I was to introduce the fireworks. This was the first time any of us had seen fireworks since 2022, but thanks to a community in New Denver made up of people that had fled Vietnam in the later 1970's, we had fireworks. Maybe not quite like they were back in the early twenties, but we had fireworks.

I stood on one of the benches overlooking the river.

" My friends, my neighbors, my new family. My heart is full tonight as we bring to a close, our Fourth of July celebration. Our country has undergone a baptism of both fire and water. And it has emerged with a united people, at least as far as we know. I remember a story I was told as a youth, that precious metals must undergo extreme heat to purify themselves. We have suffered that heat. My old mentor, Chris Bowen, told me that as a young man he had fought in Vietnam to keep those same impurities from threatening a country, but the fire never was hot enough to make us pure. My uncle fought in the war know as WWII. It again, with all the lives lost, didn't purify us. And a good part of you remember the days of the terrorism threats against our country. But still, we had no unity. At times in the early teens we became externally divided, as much so as we were during the great War of the Rebellion in the 1860's. But still, we held on. We maintained a need for freedom. Our flag was dirty and tattered, and been thrown in the dirt and picked up again by good men and women and held high. I am quite old now, and still have memories of what that flag meant. So, as you watch these fireworks tonight, keep a fire inside you for freedom. Cradle it in your heart to keep it lit. I love all of you, God bless you."

As I stepped down, Misty stood and walked forward.

"May I sing the anthem, Uncle Jeff?"

"Well, of course, Misty. Do you need music?" She shook her head no.

She stepped to the table, and faced her audience. I said, "Folks, my niece, Misty Bradley!"

Her voice came clear and strong, carried by the canyon and the night air.

"Oooohh, say, can you see? By the dawns early light........"

The first of silver spray of fireworks lit the sky behind her, a gasp went up from the crowd.

"...what's so proudly we hailed, at twilight's last gleaming."

More fireworks followed, highlighting her silhouette above us.

"Whose broad stripes and bright stars, through the perilous fight...."

I sat with tears in my eyes at the beautiful

song rendered by a strong beautiful voice. As I looked around, people were transfixed and crying unashamedly. I listened and watched.

And finally, as the fireworks subsided, came the words,

"And the Star Spangled Banner in triumph shall wave, o'er the land of the free, and the home of the brave."

Misty raised her head and said, "You are what has made this a great country. You should be proud. I will feel honored to make my new home here with you. Thank you."

For just a moment there was silence. Then everyone stood, and started to clap. And then louder and faster, then came whistles and yells that seemed to go on forever.

It was an hour before people started to drift away. Misty had people coming and thanking her for what seemed like forever.

"I turned to Damien and said, "Has she always sang like that?"

He looked at me, "I never knew!"

Russ turned to us, "Yes, I knew she could sing. She would sing to Todd and around the house, but it was always a quiet voice. I can't believe what I just heard! I think you must have inspired her Uncle Jeff."

As Marion and I crawled into bed a little later. she said, "Jeff, Misty had voice lessons as a young girl. She just fell in love with Russ and all this other stuff came down and she never did anything with it. She is interested in giving voice lessons, and we are talking about having a monthly talent show to see what else might show up."

"Good idea. Now, come here and cuddle up old lady, and stop talking so much."

"Jeff Bartlett, you are mean!"

"Uh Huh. And after dancing with all these young women tonight, I am thinking about going and finding me one."

"Yes, and after talking like that, you may have to find one. Then you have to figure out what to do with her, and we will just sit back and laugh and see how long you last!"

She turned her back and scooted over to the side of the bed and covered her head. I followed her and slipped my arms around her. She elbowed me in the ribs, and turned over and kissed me, saying, "It's a damned good thing I love you so much."

Next morning we took wagons down to the railway, or rather, we dispatched wagons to the railway. The family took the zip lines down to the bottom of the canyon, and met the wagons that had been set aside for the moving.

It was early afternoon before we reached the rail wagons, and late afternoon before our wagons was loaded. We made it back to the hotel about 11 p.m. Everyone was quite thoroughly exhausted, including myself.

Next morning, after breakfast, Damien approached me with another fellow. He said, "Jeff, I would like you to meet Ed Brauner. He was one of my neighbors up in Idaho. It was his know-how that built the rail wagons."

"Happy to meet you, Mr. Brauner. And thank you for the help in getting my family back to me."

"You are most welcome, Mr. Bartlett. I am glad we made it here, and happy to meet you. You know, this uniting was a spiritual up-lifter for us all. It was just a basic awakening that good things do happen. Not always what are expected or when you expect them, but they do happen."

"If I may call you Ed, that is very true. We have seen it happen time and again."

"And if I may call you Jeff, the reason I wanted to speak to you. Why haven't you utilized any of the old steam engines? I have seen, in Cheyenne on the way down, as well as the one here in Fort Collins. I am sure they can be brought back to life, with some work. Back near the turn of the century, I worked for the narrow gauge in Durango, Colorado. These old machines are pretty basic, and can be put to use."

"Well, Ed, we just never had anyone with any knowledge of them. If you are that man, we will throw a good amount of resources behind you."

"Consider it done. Give an old railroad man a new life."

"Where are you staying?"

"Here at the hotel for the time being. I am a single man, hotels are fine for me."

"Very good. I will send some people to see you. His name is Mike McCullom. He will get you what you need."

Later on that day, I got a message to Mike by radio and explained the plan to him. This was exciting. If this worked it would give us a new work horse.

The next two days were spent moving Russ and Misty's and Cissy and Brad's goods to The Fortress. Damien and Sandy's possessions were trucked up to New Phoenix. All the other wagons were unloaded and the inhabitants given housing and responsibilities. We took carriages up to Cherokee Park, then up the narrow dirt roads to The Fortress. The last mile or so brought back memories of my early days here. I had not taken this route in several years, due to my work at New Phoenix. As the horses strained in their harness, climbing the quarter mile hill, I was reminded of all the goods and materials that had been hauled up here in the building of mine and Nell's home.

As he drove into the compound, Brian and Danny came out welcoming us home. Both were now old men, and life had taken it's measures with them. But their minds were sharp and clear, and I always went to them for the last word of advise about any project we attempted. I introduced them to my family. They seemed over joyed to meet everyone.

The two young couples walked to the edge of the deck and peered down into the canyon from whence they had just come.

They turned and almost in unison voiced a tearful "Thank you Uncle Jeff! This is beautiful!"

"I am so happy you kids are here to claim it. I always wondered what would happen to it, since Nell and I had no issue."

I walked across the yard to the graves where Nell and Chris and Amigo lay resting.

"Nell," I said, "I brought you company. Chris, here are more young people that would have enjoyed your influence. Amigo, there are kids to play with, maybe more later, we hope. I miss all of you, I wish you could have been here to see this day."

Marion had appeared at my elbow. "Yes, you would have been able to see this old man with a smile on his face most of the time!"

About three weeks later, I stood at the crossing, where I had met Damien and watch three teams of draft horses tow a late 1800's, maybe early 1900's, steam locomotive into town and under the shed that had been built for it's restoration center. Ed had mentioned there was another in Cheyenne and one in Laramie, as well as the one that sat in downtown Fort Collins. But this would be the first and the easiest to put in working order.

August 19, 2048

I am now eighty years old. Most of the people my age have now passed on. The trials of twenty -six years ago, and the hard ships of living, shortened the lives of many. The lack of medical aid in the first fifteen years took may more. I am a lucky person to have survived. I am, for the most part, in good health, although weakened by the years. My movements have slowed somewhat, but that is the price of extended life.

Our communities grow each year. We have trains now. They are coal burners, and we have given ourselves ten years to replace the polluting monsters, or else they must be shutdown. We won't allow ourselves to make those mistakes of the past again. Our railways have reached as far northeast as Minnesota and Chicago, and the Cornbelts of Iowa and Indiana. Our food supplies grow continually every year.

We have a hospital, near old Fort Collins, on a hill that was once the equine teaching hospital of CSU! We go west to Utah. The Mormons have survived quite well, and we trade with them on many different levels. We ran a train as far south as we could go into Texas, The waters now only extend up near Waco. They are swampy for miles, making it difficult to reach open water. Everything west of the hill country seems to be dry. We haven't found people yet, but some must have survived. It is probably only a matter of time and energy. We hope to find boats and ships to explore what originally were the coastal areas at some point. The spirit of exploration has caught up our young people. That will take us forward in our new world.

Our schools are the best, from reports, of any in the country. We have come from a people almost destroyed to a people with an advancing spirit. As of yet, we have had no need of a central government. Pray that we never need one. A central government has tendencies to so isolate itself from it's people that the people's need become unimportant. Then it becomes an entity that is only self serving, and centers on it's own needs. I could cite examples of this, but as thinking individuals, I leave you to research it yourselves.

It was beyond the scope of America's forefathers to see how far the arms of America would reach in its latter days. All they knew was governments of the past, which were set up by reigning minorities to regulate the majorities. They didn't realize that those majorities needed only self sustaining goals, and local councils to keep them focused. All they truly needed was the right to *'life, liberty, and the pursuit of happiness'.*

Most of our Founding Fathers had expired before our westward nation had expanded across the wide Mississippi. That being said, what they really had no idea about was the industrial revolution and the explosion of technology that would occur in the end of the 19th century and the beginning of the 20th. The world shrunk to a third of it's original size and suddenly America's arms reached almost all the way around it. Suddenly, society was not ruled by how far a man could walk, or ride a horse, or how much goods he could put on a wagon and lumber across a prairie, or how the winds would prevail for a sailing ship to cross the ocean. Soon, an Iron Horse breathing smoke and fire, with a cargo of a dozen wagon trains, would fly across those plains, bringing settlers and pioneers as fast as they could breed families. No care was taken in those old Congresses to curb the dissension that would arise form an exploding nation and population. And soon, America would be brought to it's knees by a great Civil War. One would think we would learn from that, don't you think?

As our communities increased and we started to grow, great care had to be taken to keep the same mistakes from occurring again. But how?

August 19, 2048

A beautiful fall morning in new Phoenix. I arose about seven and went for a short walk down to the Cache de Poudre. I loved mornings on the river. The trout were lively this morning, jumping and catching insects out of the air, flashing silver in drops of water. A herd of deer drank from the river on the opposite side about 50 yards upstream. I sat on one of the benches we had placed there some years ago for just this purpose. Our teachers would bring their students down and sit them here, and required them to be quiet and watch nature around them. Sometimes one of our Arapahoe friends would come and quietly point out small creatures going about their daily lives.

I sat and pondered what direction could we take as leaders to keep our growth from heading into an uncontrolled torrent that would allow those people by nature who would try to prostitute it for their own gain at the expense of others. My musings were shattered by

"Happy Birthday to you! Happy birthday to you! Happy birthday Uncle Jeff! Happy birthday to you!"

Sung by the chorus of Damiens' family, accompanied by Mike and Shelly, the two Daves' and their spouses, Arne, and a whole host of my friends and neighbors, as well as Marion.

They has slipped up on me as I sat oblivious to the rest of the world lost in my own thoughts. It was a heartwarming thing, to have all these dear people make the effort to do this for me.

I pulled my handkerchief from my jacket pocket, and wiped my eyes.

"Thank you dear ones. I had clean forgotten what today was. When one has had this many birthdays, one has a notion to forget them. But this is a remarkable milestone to reach, and to be surrounded by so many who care. Thank you so much."

I now had another niece belonging to Russ and Misty. And Cissy and Brad had just presented me a new nephew. The first was Diana Nell Bradley, and the second Jefferson Bradley Jones. I was over joyed. My friends helped to escort me back to the community center which was full of more neighbors, all wishing me a happy birthday. It seems they had set the whole day aside for my entertainment. So my eightieth solar return was filled with love and friendship, singing and dancing and recitals, and visitors - lots of visitors. At the end of the day Mike stood and walked to the head of the room.

"Jeff, here is something that has come some distance for you, although they are as old and some older than you. Those people that you visited some years ago in Telluride haven't for gotten you. Here is a letter they have asked me to read to you.

"Dear Mr. Bartlett,

The human entity has evolved over the millennia to a functional being. But it needs all parts to function. It needs a brain to power it, you had that. And we helped to fill that wonderful brain with ideas. Next, it needs a heart to give meaning and feeling and the energy to put those ideas to fruition. And, Mr Bartlett, you had that great heart. Selfless in it's desire to serve your community, open to accept others to make your community grow. Next, it needed broad shoulders to carry the load of responsibility. You never staggered under that huge weight. But from the wisdom of your mind, the love in your heart, and the strength you exhibited, came many sets of hands to create the success that you have been a part of in your communities. Congratulations on this day.

Although not in body, we are here with you in spirit."

I had remained in contact with these great friends, especially Du Hua. I knew how busy their lives were, and knew their dedication. I was humbled by them taking this time for me.

I sat for a moment, speechless, not knowing what to say. A jumble of thoughts washed through my mind. I felt that I was not deserving of this praise. I had never sought it. My life had been planned to be a quiet reclusive on on my mountain in the foothills of the Colorado Rockies. Others had given of their labors. They deserved this more than me. Finally, I stood, slowly.

"Forgive me, my friends. I am Jeff Bartlett. I grew up somewhat of an orphan on the streets of Austin, Texas. I was a petty thief, and quite a neer-do-well in my youth. It is hard to listen to words such as these spoken about me, they humble me to my knees. I don't want praise for what has happened here. Others have worked hard, probably harder than I. What I have done, I have done for my friends and now my family. I wish only for that acceptance. If I were to ask anything of you, it would only be that our new world could grow as it is - uncomplicated, without avarice or greed among it's inhabitants. To grow with honesty toward each other, and the well being of the whole foremost in each community members mind. This morning, before my family surprised me at the rivers edge, I watched a herd of deer grazing and drinking from the river. Each drink of water, each blade of grass, was shared equally with them. My attention was then turned to a colony of ants busy building their warehouses and stuffing them for the cold winter coming. They were busy carrying loads climbing over each other. If a load was too heavy for one ant, another took up the load, but the job never slowed. That is the way I want to see us work together.

"I would like to find a spot and build a huge deck high up where we could go and contemplate the night skies as early man did. Not that it is needed to discover new things about our universe, but to give us perspective in our lives. How the simple things are so important. I only worry, after seeing our world destroyed, that we will forget these lessons and allow us to go astray again. Thank you for a wonderful day. I hope to celebrate with you many more times."

For my eightieth birthday present I took a train ride out to the east. We had nothing but an engine, a passenger lounge car, a Pullman, and a empty flat and an extra coal car and two box cars with horses and tack and feed and a carriage for the old men and women. We traveled across Kansas, taking our time, watching the rails ahead. We were cautious of trestles and the road in general, but it was still strong. We inspected then crossed the Missouri River at Kansas City, then again just before we got to Columbia. But it was long after that, that the ground became unstable. We packed some stores and unloaded horses, carriage, and gear, and set out looking for the Mississippi River. We found that a huge range of hills had sprung up, some 60 miles west of St. Louis, similar to what

Crowley's Ridge had appeared after the 1812 New Madrid quake. The Missouri had rerouted itself and ran into the Mississippi some forty miles farther north. The closest we were able to get was about thirty miles. St. Louis was rubble, grown over by a quarter century of wild vegetation. But the arch still stood, visible in the distance, as if it was saying, *I will not yield*.

We camped for a night near the old remains of a sign saying, *Wright City, Missouri*. I wondered, is this what Lewis and Clark saw in the first part of the 1800's? We found no people 'till we recrossed the Missouri at Kansas City. Then we began to see small groups appear on the sides of the railroad. We would stop and listen to their stories, and promise them we would make return trips and open trade with them. Small communities appeared all across Kansas. Some told us that when we had steamed across, they figured we would return so they set watchmen to wait for us.

The excitement from finding people in Kansas motivated us to send out more probes, and by doing so we found other points of population, other pockets of talents and energy to help us build our new world. In September, after school had enrolled, Marion and I went back to The Fortress for a visit with my nieces and nephews. We stayed for a couple of weeks. I spent a large part of the time sitting on my deck over the canyon; writing, studying history and trying to apply suggestion to what time had taught us. I have reached a point when my love of cannabis has all but diminished. No longer does it make my mind expand and creative thoughts pour in, like a bowl overflowing with water. It seemed to happen anyway. It seemed that is the gods' joke on mankind.

When finally you have mastered your mind, and have learned the priorities of life, and know how to direct those creative energies, then the gods jerk your feet from under you. By weakening you physically, taking the spring from your stride, making just standing a painful endeavor, dimming your eyes and stopping your ears!

But never mind that, we will just take a little longer, but will not stop. As I would sit in the afternoon looking out to the north, I would find my self taking 'old man naps'. But during these naps, things another old man taught me kept appearing in my mind. Ideas that I might not have ever thought of myself. I would drift back to earlier days and pictures of myself making bad decisions would haunt me, causing me to sometimes wake with a start, and scramble to write them down before they would fade like a heavy smoke in a breeze.

Then I would dream of those early days with Nell, watching her beautiful body as she waded in the waterfall and worked in the greenhouse, sometimes in her birthday suit. Remembering the days and nights of making love in any one of numbers of places here on our mountaintop, including this very deck. Most times I would wake from these dreams with tears in my eyes. If there is justice in this universe, we will get to go back and live with these loved ones in our next life. I wondered often, how long will it be before I have the answer to this question? I thought, not so very long!

Marion and I walked a lot showing the family places that were favorites of ours. We took a small carriage and went to the water fall. It was enjoyable watching the kids play in the cold water, screaming as they ran under the icy waters of the falls. I would look up and could almost see Nell looking down with a smile on her face. Marion knew what I was thinking. She smiled and said, "This was her favorite place."

I answered, "Yes it was." I pointed at the small grassy spot in the sun across from the falls, "There is where I first saw the two of you together. The sight is burned into my memory. It was a picture of love between two beautiful people. I will never forget it. It was not my desire to interrupt it, but it was the start of those terrible times."

She smiled, "I had never experienced anything so exciting in my life. I had always loved her, but here it took on a whole new meaning. No, I will never forget it either. We understood. I miss her as you do."

We walked in the forest, showing the children the place we called the 'Fairy Grotto'. We watched the herds of deer and elk graze the meadows, and at night listened to the bull elks trumpeting around us. We watched the stars, and for brief periods of time would forget our ages. We laughed at silly jokes and kept my family awake at night, until I was sure we had worn out our welcome. Finally, after about three weeks we bade our goodbyes and caught a morning coach back to New Phoenix.

After a good night sleep that night I arose that morning to walk out my door and find Arne and David and some young men standing around an old Volkswagen Jetta, of about the early 2000's vintage. It was a diesel engine car, and it was sitting in the road running. I hurried over, filled with wonder and questions.

"Good morning Jeff," was echoed several times.

"Where did this come from?" I asked excitedly.

One young man, by the name of Steve Swift, answered, saying that he had found it inside a garage in Fort Collins, and that he had tinkered with it for years trying to make it run on hemp oil that we were distilling for different uses. He further remarked that he had dissembled almost everything at least twice and re-assembled before achieving success. He had kept a journal of his work so that possibly in the future the process could be shortened. He also remarked that the biggest problem was tires, as all the rubber was now becoming so rotten, he had to replace all four tires on the way up to New Phoenix.

"Gentlemen, this a real boon. Not only for transportation but for industry as well. With engines such as these we can race forward, literally, in many areas. Tell everyone to keep their eyes open for these little autos, and Arne, try some of the truck engines and see if they can be modified. This is huge, I am really excited!

And, Arne, sometime back I remember before Chaos, maybe 2014 or '15, there was some company starting to make wheels that were not inflated , see if you can dig up information on these."

All this before breakfast, I wondered what else the new day would bring. As I went back to my cottage, I met Marion standing in the doorway.

"Is that what I think it was?"

"Yep."

"I never thought I would ever see that again."

"Nor I. But we sometimes have the tendencies to underestimate the younger generations and their capabilities."

"Yes, my dear, we do. And that is a bad habit!"

After breakfast, I knocked on Damiens' door.

He answered, I went inside, and sat and told him of my morning discovery. He almost jumped off his chair.

"Jeff, I have two men in my group - a father and a son - that were diesel mechanics. We need to go see them."

" I am ready when you are!"

We said bye to our spouses and had Marion radio down to the bottom of the canyon and have a carriage waiting for us. An hour and a half later found us boarding a carriage for the short ride to the community that had been set aside for the Idaho families.

Robert Poole had worked for a truck diesel shop in Spokane for many years. His son had worked in auto diesel for some time as well. Both men were excited when I told them about the little Volkswagen. They agreed that it was very plausible, that indeed, one of the early diesel engines of the 20th century had been designed to run on hemp. I told them to come up to New Phoenix and see David and Arne, and they would see about getting them a shop set up. So much would have to be done on the autos. Without petroleum lubrication would have to be rethought, as well as many other things. But it was all possible. We took our carriage back to the foot of the canyon and took the lift back up reaching home late, just before dark. I was much distressed with fatigue, and I could see my brother was tired as well. We bid our so longs and headed for the comforts of our own cabins.

May 12, 2055

I am in my 87th year. Thirty-thee years ago we were about to experience the most devastating set of circumstances that had ever happened to our country. Now, we have risen. Not to our former self, but to a new level, one more environmental, more evenly governed, more educated than before. The last five years have been miraculous. We have autos, not many, but there will be more. We can go longer distances, faster. We are developing our medical skills, and saving more lives. We have developed a type of currency that allows us to trade with more people, but we are guarding against inflation. We watched it kill our last world. We have fine-tuned our governing force, making it a duty, and a privilege, but not allowing it to become a career.

In the last year, more of my friends have past on, making me long for their company again. As I pen this, I am waiting for my carriage. I am going to meet some old friends, that I thought I would never see again - Katherine from Telluride, and Dr. Du Hua, a friend, and a Pharmacist. He has created new medicines, and brought back to life old ones, that were much need to keep our people alive. We lost many in those early days, to fevers and infections, cancers. My beloved Nell fell victim to such. We had no treatments then, not even pain relievers to much extent.

Now, this evening, I get to see these old friends again.

When the time came, I was taken to the community center, to a small theater, with seating that is Colosseum-like, being low in the center and higher in the rear. It is an amazing place. We can talk and even people in the rear can hear quiet easily. However, tonight we have a speaker system.

A crowd has already gathered, and as I am lead into the center with four or five chairs and a small table in the center, a voice comes over the speakers.

"Ladies and Gentlemen, Mr. Jeff Bartlett."

As I turned to acknowledge the voice, everyone stood and applauded for several minutes. Within a moment or so, I looked up to see a lady in white being wheeled into the area by a young monk in saffron robes. I recognized her and held out my hands as the announcer spoke,

"Ladies and Gentlemen, Ms. Catherine Noble.

She is one of those we have so often referred to as the Sages from Telluride." Again, the crowd applauded respectfully. Catherine raised her hand and wave to the crowd, smiling as she did. I came to her side and took her hand and knelt, embracing her.

I said, "I am so happy to see you again, my friend."

"Jeff, what I see here is awesome and inspiring. You should be very proud."

"Catherine, it has been a compilation of work by a lot of people. Those you see around you, particularly on the lower seats, especially deserve your praise."

We were interrupted by the announcer once more.

"Ladies and Gentlemen, Dr. Du Hua!"

Again, applause, but not so much as most

411

didn't know who he was. Very well, I would see to that. I walked to him and embraced him. He was a bit older than I, but still bore himself erect and strong.

"Du Hua, I am so proud to meet you again, it has been years."

"Yes, my brother, it has been long. But we have been blessed for it to be."

We took our seats around the table. Some people came out and attached our microphones.

The announcer spoke.

"Folks, tonight we are so privileged to have to speak three individuals without whom the out come of this and most other communities might have been much different. I am going to ask Mr. Bartlett to introduce his friends, then we will have each of them speak about what has happened to them and what they see for our future. Mr. Bartlett?"

"Ladies and Gentlemen, and all you children, for I see many out there this beautiful evening. My first guest is Catherine Noble. Catherine and her friends came to our rescue several years ago by holding classes for our students, in many different fields of endeavor - from medicine , to mathematics, to so many other things. We had smart students, they made them smarter. We gave them clay, and they shaped that clay into beautiful, useful vessels. Without them we might be still wandering the darkness with nary a candle to light our way. They were a beacon, literally shining on a hill.

"I will give her something left to say and introduce my other friend. In doing so, Sam Jackson, up there in the third row, I see your beautiful daughter with you. Stand up, dear." She stood. "You remember Sam when she had that terrible fever a couple of years ago?" Sam nodded. "Well, this is the man that created that medicine that saved her life. And you, up there in the fifth row, with that blood infection, he saved you too. Dr. Du Hua is a pharmacist, he makes medicine. He is a true savior, but he wasn't always.

He was born in the 60's in Vietnam, during that horrible war. He grew up under the yoke of Communism. But he was determined to escape it and his subdued country. He tried at least nine times, failing each time. But he wouldn't give up. He finally apprenticed himself to a marine diesel engineer to learn the trade and to have an excuse to be on a boat. Three more times he tried, losing everything each time. Finally, they succeeded, only to be nearly killed at sea several times. They were rescued and taken to a refugee camp. To shorten the story, his indomitable spirit got him to America. He educated himself, against all odds. He joined the U.S. Navy, served proudly, and afterwards, with extreme hardship, went back to school and become a Pharmacist. Folks, he is a real hero. I met him the first time as a youngster in Houston, just after he arrived. He was lucky enough to have been in Telluride, when Chaos happened. Catherine and Dr. Hua, take a bow."

This was followed by a huge round of

applause and a standing ovation.

Each of my guests were allowed time to speak and voice their appreciation of events happening all over our state, and tell of their past. Catherine spoke of the university that she was president of, how she was trying to take educations to a new level, and make it available for all those that were willing to work for it. No free rides was her motto. She told of the successes, and how new professors were coming from students. Of how education had been tempered by politics, and how we could never allow it to happen again.

Dr. Du Hua thanked me for my introduction, saying that twice his country had been taken from him, but he would never allow it to totally slip from his grasp. He spoke about he had never thought about him having courage, he only thought about how much he wanted freedom. He said that he thought that must be the answer to courage - it must be an unquenchable desire for something that keeps you moving forward. He closed in saying that he was now teaching medicine and was looking for good students.

As the question and answer session opened, I got the first from a young lady who introduced herself as Toni from Goodland, Kansas.

"Mr. Jeff, you are admired by everyone I meet. What were you like when you were my age, and what made you the person you are now?"

"Toni, you are about 17?" She nodded yes. "I was an outlaw, a street kid, headed for trouble. What made me what I am today? I ran into someone who cared for me and believed in me. I made a decision, and set some goals."

"Ms. Catherine," it was a man in his mid-forties, "how do you teach your children that education is necessary?"

"You don't teach them that education is necessary, you show them the limits of their lives with out education. You try to instill in them a quest for knowledge. Then they will see that education provides the answer to their goals."

"Dr. Du Hua, I am only 21 years old. Sir, I know nothing of your country, or what happened there,. Does your country still exist?"

"Young Sir, I would love to answer your question, but my answer would take the entire night, and we still would not finish. Many years ago I wrote a book that tells the story of me and my country. There are copies of it still available. See me later and I will make it available to you, and thank you for caring."

"Mr. Jeff, I have heard of you since I was a small boy, but know little of your life. Is there a book about you? It would be of benefit for some of us to know of the events that happened before and leading up to the disaster. Many of us are too young to remember. We get bits and pieces, but not all."

"Um, hmmm, no, not at present. But perhaps I

will make that a project if you think it will help."

It was an instant applause that lasted for several seconds.

"Very well! You asked for it!"

We answered questions for about an hour, but, I could see my friends were getting tired, so we closed. We went to a smaller meeting room in the lodge and had a late dinner and talked for several hours more. We decided that memoirs of all of us should be written and published, and that should include anyone over the age of 75. We decided it should be projects for our colleges, to collect and publish these stories.

Next morning, we had a breakfast together. Then it was my pleasure to give my friends and their companions a guided tour of New Phoenix and our garden and greenhouses. I wished that we could have gone to The Fortress, but I realized they still had a long trip ahead, so our goodbyes were said. Each of us parted, knowing that the possibility of not meeting again in this life was quite real, but it was not mentioned. Catherine was the first to go. We each remarked to the other that it was a shame that we didn't meet earlier in life. But as she said, "Perhaps we might not have been the same people that we have become, and the appreciation might not have been there." A wonderfully wise woman.

My friend Dr. Du Hua was harder. Although we had not spent much time in our lives together, I felt he was one of my oldest friends. He had been an inspiration since I had first met him. Now, he was leaving, and time was not on our side. But, as I watched him disappear down the road, I thought of him and Chris. They never met, but were the two most important men of my life. The old saying was true, '*When ever the student is ready, a teacher will appear*'.

I turned away from my memories. I must put together this story, my story. It was only a simple story, of a young runaway boy in Texas trying to survive without a family to guide him, making mistakes, sometimes paying a high price.

Getting lucky, and being able to live a long and wonderful life. Even better, people wanted it to be told. Very well, I will do it.

I waked across the street and found a group of my old friends sitting down to a late lunch in the Old Lodge. Mike, the Two Davids, Arne, and a couple more.

"Mike, if Shelly is available, I need to speak with her. I need her help with this book that I have promised."

"Sure thing, Jeff!"

October 29, 2055

Last night we sat under the stars, and I had about 20 kids ranging form nine to seventeen siting with me. They wanted stories from the past, so I told them stories of Austin in the late 80's and the 90's, of being a young person there. I told them of the festivals, on 6th Street, and about Guadalupe Street and all the antics that used to prevail. We talked about the big

Renaissance Festival in a little town called Todd Mission, and the thousands of people that would come there every year. I told them of the traffic that would snarl the roads, and how people would sit for hours on their way here and there. About the giant airplanes that took people all over the world in a few hours. I talked about the many different cultures that mixed in our world. I tried to think of only the positive. I talked of being young and in love with a beautiful girl. They listened attentively, and went away thoughtful and silent. They have to build their world, they will build it better. And someday, when they are old, they will tell their stories to other young ones. It has been that way since time began.

For the past months my two young scribes, Lilly and Patty, have been recording my life, as I have told it, from my earliest memories to the time just some what before Chaos occurred. We have finished with that. I have enjoyed the interaction with these two young people. Their jokes about my naivety as a young man. And many questions, without those maybe half the story might not have been told. I am ready to start the second half of the story, dear reader. I am ready to tell you how a world can fall apart, how it can survive and and be born anew. I will start with my thoughts shortly after the event happened. I hope you will enjoy the story and heed my warning, because history repeats itself.

Well here goes.

After Texas sank, I started remembering more of the things that the Old Man talked about. No one actually believed that half the United States would just up and disappear, but the Old Man had mentioned that it was a possibility. Yeah, but he was just an old man. I thought he was pretty cool though. He would stand up to anyone. He hated to see people waste their lives following false ideals.

But when Texas started mimicking the Titanic, I realized just maybe he might be right about some other things that he expounded. I was about 22 when I met him. Funny, I don't remember exactly the first time I saw him, but I sure remember the first time I became aware of him. It was 1990. Remember, I was 22. I was pretty sure that I had accumulated all the knowledge that a young male human would ever need, and I was probably invulnerable. Yeah, right.....